SO BRIGHT THE VISION

There was a strange creaking noise from somewhere and I glanced hurriedly around to find out what it was. I found out, all right.

Over on one corner, my favourite chair was slowly and deliberately and weirdly coming apart. The upholstery nails were smoothly rising from the edging of the fabric — rising as if by their own accord — and, dropping to the floor with tiny patterings. As I watched, a bolt fell to the floor and one leg bent underneath the chair and the chair toppled over. The upholstery nails kept right on coming out.

And as I stood there watching this, I felt the anger draining out of me and a fear come dribbling in to take its place. I started to get cold all over and I could feel the gooseflesh rising . . .

Clifford D. Simak

So Bright
the Vision

MAGNUM BOOKS
Methuen Paperbacks Ltd

A Magnum Book

SO BRIGHT THE VISION
ISBN 0 417 02360 X

First published 1968
by Ace Books, Inc.
Magnum edition published 1978

THE GOLDEN BUGS
copyright © 1960 by Mercury Press, Inc.,
LEG. FORST.
copyright © 1958 for *Infinity Science Fiction*
SO BRIGHT THE VISION
copyright © 1956 for *Fantastic Universe*
GALACTIC CHEST
copyright © 1956 for *Original Science Fiction*

Magnum Books are published
by Methuen Paperbacks Ltd
11 New Fetter Lane, London EC4P 4EE
Made and printed in Great Britain
by Richard Clay (The Chaucer Press) Ltd.,
Bungay, Suffolk

TABLE OF CONTENTS

THE GOLDEN BUGS

It started as a lousy day.

Arthur Belsen, across the alley, turned on his orchestra at six o'clock and brought me sitting up in bed.

I'm telling you, Belsen makes his living as an engineer, but music is his passion. And since he is an engineer, he's not content to leave well enough alone. He had to mess around.

A year or two before he'd had the idea of a robotic symphony, and the man has talent, you have to give him that. He went to work on this idea and designed machines that could read—not only play, but read—music from a tape, and he built a machine to transcribe the tapes. Then he built a lot of these music machines in his basement workshop.

And he tried them out!

It was experimental work, quite understandably, and there was redesigning and adjusting to be done, and Belsen was finicky about the performance that each machine turned out. So he tried them out a lot—and loudly—not being satisfied until he had the instrumentation just the way he thought it should be.

There had been some idle talk in the neighborhood about a lynching party, but nothing came of it. That's the trouble, one of the troubles, with this neighborhood of ours—they'll talk an arm off you, but never do a thing.

As yet no one could see an end to all the Belsen racket. It had taken him better than a year to work up the percussion section and that was bad enough. But now he'd started on the strings and that was even worse.

Helen sat up in bed beside me and put her hands up to her ears, but she couldn't keep from hearing. Belsen had it turned up loud, to get, as he would tell you, the feel of it.

7

By this time, I figured, he probably had the entire neighborhood awake.

"Well, that's it," I said, starting to get up.

"You want me to get breakfast?"

"You might as well," I said. "No one's going to get any sleep with that thing turned on."

While she started breakfast, I headed for the garden back of the garage to see how the dahlias might be faring. I don't mind telling you I was delighted with those dahlias. It was nearly fair time and there were some of them that would be at bloom perfection just in time for showing.

I started for the garden, but I never got there. That's the way it is in this neighborhood. A man will start to do something and never get it done because someone always catches him and wants to talk a while.

This time it was Dobby. Dobby is Dr. Darby Wells, a venerable old codger with white chin whiskers, and he lives next door. We all call him Dobby and he doesn't mind a bit, for in a way it's a badge of tribute to the man. At one time Dobby had been an entomologist of some repute at the university and it had been his students who had hung the name on him. It was no corruption of his regular name, but stemmed rather from his one-time interest in mud-dauber wasps.

But now Dobby was retired, with nothing in the world to do except hold long and aimless conversations with anyone he could manage to nail down.

As soon as I caught sight of him, I knew I was sunk.

"I think it's admirable," said Dobby, leaning on his fence and launching into full-length discussion as soon as I was in voice distance, "for a man to have a hobby. But I submit it's inconsiderate of him to practice it so noisily at the crack of dawn."

"You mean that," I said, making a thumb at the Belsen house, from which the screeching and the caterwauling still issued in full force.

"Exactly," said Dobby, combing his white chin whiskers with an air of grave deliberation. "Now, mind me, not for a moment would I refuse the man the utmost admiration...."

"Admiration?" I demanded. There are occasions when I have a hard time understanding Dobby. Not so much because

8

of the pontifical way in which he talks as because of the way he thinks.

"Precisely," Dobby told me. "Not for his machines, although they are electronic marvels, but for the way in which he engineers his tapes. The machine that he rigged up to turn out those tapes is a most versatile contraption. Sometimes it seems to be almost human."

"When I was a boy," I said, "we had player pianos and the pianos ran on tapes."

"Yes, Randall, you are right," admitted Dobby; "the principle was there, but the execution—think of the execution! All those old pianos had to do was tinkle merrily along, but Belsen has worked into his tapes the most delicate nuances."

"I must have missed them nuances," I told him, without any charity at all. "All I've heard is racket."

We talked about Belsen and his orchestra until Helen called me in for breakfast.

I had no sooner sat down than she dragged out her grievance list.

"Randall," she said, with determination, "the kitchen is positively crawling with grease ants again. They're so small you can hardly see them and all at once they're into everything."

"I thought you got rid of them," I said.

"I did. I tracked them to their nest and poured boiling water into it. But this time it's up to you."

"Sure thing," I promised. "I'll do it right away."

"That's what you said last time."

"I was ready to," I told her, "but you beat me to it."

"And that isn't all," she said. "There are those wasps up in the attic louvers. They stung the little Montgomery girl the other day."

She was getting ready to say more, but just then Billy, our eleven year old, came stumbling down the stairs.

"Look, Dad," he cried excitedly, holding out a small-size plastic box. "I have one here I've never seen before."

I didn't have to ask one what. I knew it was another insect. Last year it had been stamp collecting and this year it was insects—and that's another thing about having an idle entomologist for a next door neighbor.

I took the box without enthusiasm.

9

"A ladybug," I said.

"No, it's not," said Billy. "It's too big to be a ladybug. And the spots are different and the color is all wrong. This one is gold and a ladybug is orange."

"Well, look it up," I said, impatiently. The kid will do anything to keep away from reading.

"I did," said Billy. "I looked all through the book and I couldn't find it."

"Oh, for goodness sakes," snapped Helen, "sit down and eat your breakfast. It's bad enough to be overrun with ants and wasps without you spending all your time catching other bugs."

"But, Mom, it's educational," protested Billy. "That's what Dr. Wells says. He says there are seven hundred thousand known families of insects. . . ."

"Where did you find it, son?" I asked, a bit ashamed of how we both were jumping on him.

"Right in my room," said Billy.

"In the house!" screamed Helen. "Ants aren't bad enough. . . ."

"Soon as I get through eating, I'll show it to Dr. Wells."

"Now, don't you pester Dobby."

"I hope he pesters him a lot," Helen said, tight-lipped. "It was Dobby who got him started on this foolishness."

I handed back the box and Billy put it down beside his plate and started in on breakfast.

"Randall," Helen said, taking up her third point of complaint. "I don't know what I'm going to do with Nora."

Nora was the cleaning woman. She came in twice a week.

"What did she do this time?"

"It's what she doesn't do. She simply will not dust. She just waves a cloth around and that's all there is to it. She won't move a lamp or vase."

"Well, get someone else," I said.

"Randall, you don't know what you're talking about. Cleaning women are hard to find and you can't depend on them. I was talking to Amy . . ."

I listened and made the appropriate replies. I've heard it all before.

As soon as I finished breakfast, I took off for the office. It was too early to see any prospects, but I had some policies to write up and some other work to do and I could use the extra hour or two.

Helen phoned me shortly after noon and she was exasperated.

"Randall," she said, without preamble, "someone has dumped a boulder in the middle of the garden."

"Come again?" I said.

"You know. A big rock. It squashed down all the dahlias."

"Dahlias!" I yipped.

"And the funny thing about it is there aren't any tracks. It would take a truck to move a rock that big and ..."

"Now, let's take this easy. How big, exactly, is this boulder?"

"It's almost as tall as I am."

"It's impossible!" I stormed. Then I tried to calm myself. "It's a joke," I said. "Someone played a joke."

I searched my mind for someone who might have done it and I couldn't think of anyone who'd go to all the trouble involved in that sort of joke. There was George Montgomery, but George was a sobersides. And Belsen, but Belsen was too wrapped up in music to be playing any jokes. And Dobby—it was inconceivable he'd ever play a joke.

"Some joke!" said Helen.

Nobody in the neighborhood, I told myself, would have done a trick like that. Everyone knew I was counting on those dahlias to win me some more ribbons.

"I'll knock off early," I told her, "and see what can be done about it."

Although I knew there was precious little that could be done about it—just haul the thing away.

"I'll be over at Amy's," Helen said. "I'll try to get home early."

I went out and saw another prospect, but I didn't do too well. All the time I was thinking of the dahlias.

I knocked off work in the middle of the afternoon and bought a spray-can of insecticide at a drugstore. The label claimed it was effective against ants, roaches, wasps, aphids and a host of other pests.

At home, Billy was sitting on the steps.

"Hello, son. Nothing much to do?"

"Me and Tommy Henderson played soldier for a while, but we got tired of it."

I put the insecticide on the kitchen table, then headed for the garden. Billy trailed listlessly behind me.

The boulder was there, squarely in the middle of the dahlia patch, and every bit as big as Helen said it was. It was a funny looking thing, not just a big slab-sided piece of rock, but a freckled looking job. It was a washed-out red and almost a perfect globe.

I walked around it, assessing the damage. There were a few of the dahlias left, but the better ones were gone. There were no tracks, no indication of how the rock might have gotten where it was. It lay a good thirty feet from the alleyway and someone might have used a crane to hoist it off a truck bed, but that seemed most unlikely, for a heavy nest of utility wires ran along the alley.

I went up to the boulder and had a good, close look at it. The whole face of it was pitted with small, irregular holes, none of them much deeper than half an inch, and there were occasional smooth patches, with the darker luster showing, as if some part of the original surface had been knocked off. The darker, smoother patches had the shine of highly polished wax, and I remembered something from very long ago—when a one-time pal of mine had been a momentary rock collector.

I bent a little closer to one of the smooth, waxy surfaces and it seemed to me that I could see the hint of wavy lines running in the stone.

"Billy," I asked, "would you know an agate if you saw one?"

"Gosh, Dad, I don't know. But Tommy would. He is a sort of rockhound. He's hunting all the time for different kinds of rocks."

He came up close, and looked at one of the polished surfaces. He wet his thumb against his tongue and rubbed it across the waxy surface to bring out the satin of the stone.

"I don't know," he said, "but I think it is."

He backed off a ways and stared at the boulder with a new respect.

"Say, Dad, if it really is an agate—if it is one big agate, I mean, it would be worth a lot of money, wouldn't it?"

12

"I don't know. I suppose it might be."

"A million dollars, maybe."

I shook my head. "Not a million dollars."

"I'll go get Tommy, right away," he said.

He went around the garage like a flash and I could hear him running down the driveway, hitting out for Tommy's place.

I walked around the boulder several times and tried to estimate its weight, but I had no knowledge I could go on.

I went back to the house and read the directions on the can of insecticide. I uncapped and tested it and the sprayer worked.

So I got down on my knees in front of the threshold of the kitchen door and tried to find the path the ants were using to come in. I couldn't see any of them right away, but I knew from past experience that they are little more than specks and almost transparent in the bargain and mighty hard to see.

A glittery motion in one corner of the kitchen caught my eye and I wheeled around. A glob of golden shimmer was running on the floor, keeping close to the baseboard and heading for the cabinet underneath the kitchen sink.

It was another of the outsize ladybugs.

I aimed the squirt can at it and let it have a burst, but it kept right on and vanished underneath the cabinet.

With the bug gone, I resumed looking for the ants and found no sign of them. There were none coming in the door. Or going out, for that matter. There were none on the sink or the work table space.

So I went around the corner of the house to size up Operation Wasp. It would be a sticky one, I knew. The nest was located in the attic louver and would be hard to get at. Standing off and looking at it, I decided the only thing to do was wait until night, when I could be sure all the wasps were in the nest. Then I'd put up a ladder and climb up and let them have it, then get out as fast as I could manage without breaking my fool neck.

It was a piece of work that I frankly had no stomach for, but I knew from the tone of Helen's voice at the breakfast table there was no ducking it.

There were a few wasps flying around the nest, and as I watched a couple of them dropped out of the nest and tumbled to the ground.

13

Wondering what was going on, I stepped a little closer and then I saw the ground was littered with dead or dying wasps. Even as I watched, another wasp fell down and lay there, twisting and squirming.

I circled around a bit to try to get a better look at whatever might be happening. But I could make out nothing except that every now and then another wasp fell down.

I told myself it was all right with me. If something was killing off the wasps it would save me the job of getting rid of them.

I was turning around to take the insecticide back to the kitchen when Billy and Tommy Henderson came panting in excitement from the backyard.

"Mr. Marsden," Tommy said, "that rock out there is an agate. It's a banded agate."

"Well, now, that's fine," I said.

"But you don't understand," cried Tommy. "No agate gets that big. Especially not a banded agate. They call them Lake Superior agates and they don't ever get much bigger than your fist."

That did it. I jerked swiftly to attention and went pelting around the house to have another look at the boulder in the garden. The boys came pounding on behind me.

That boulder was a lovely thing. I put out my hand and stroked it. I thought how lucky I was that someone had plopped it in my garden. I had forgotten all about the dahlias.

"I bet you," Tommy told me, his eyes half as big as saucers, "that you could get a lot of money for it."

I won't deny that approximately the same thought had been going through my mind.

I put out my hand and pushed against it, just to get the solid and substantial feel of it.

And as I pushed, it rocked slightly underneath the pressure!

Astonished, I pushed a little harder, and it rocked again.

Tommy stood bug-eyed. "That's funny, Mr. Marsden. By rights, it hadn't ought to move. It must weigh several tons. You must be awfully strong."

"I'm not strong," I told him. "Not as strong as that."

I tottered back to the house and put away the insecticide, then went out and sat down on the steps to do some worrying.

There was no sign of the boys. They probably had run

swiftly off to spread the news through the neighborhood.

If that thing was an agate, as Tommy said it was—if it really was one tremendous agate, then it would be a fantastic museum piece and might command some money. But if it was an agate, why was it so light? No ten men, pushing on it, should have made it budge.

I wondered, too, just what my rights would be if it should actually turn out to be an agate. It was on my property and it should be mine. But what if someone came along and claimed it?

And there was this other thing: How had it gotten there to start with?

I was all tied up in knots with my worrying when Dobby came trundling around the corner of the house and sat down on the steps beside me.

"Lots of extraordinary things going on," he said. "I hear you have an agate boulder in the garden."

"That's what Tommy Henderson tells me. I suppose that he should know. Billy tells me he's a rockhound."

Dobby scratched at his whiskers. "Great things, hobbies," he said. "Especially for kids. They learn a lot from them."

"Yeah," I said without enthusiasm.

"Your son brought me an insect for identification after breakfast this morning."

"I told him not to bother you."

"I am glad he brought it," Dobby said. "It was one I'd never seen before."

"It looked like a ladybug."

"Yes," Dobby agreed, "there is *some* resemblance. But I'm not entirely certain—well, fact of the matter is, I'm not even sure that it is an insect. To tell the truth, it resembles a turtle in many ways more than it does an insect. There is an utter lack of bodily segmentation, such as you'd find in any insect. The exoskeleton is extremely hard and the head and legs are retractible and it has no antennae."

He shook his head in some perplexity. "I can't be sure, of course. Much more extensive examination would be necessary before an attempt could be made at classifying it. You didn't happen to find any more of them, did you?"

"I saw one running on the floor not so long ago."

15

"Would you mind, next time you see one, grabbing it for me?"

"Not at all," I said. "I'll try to get you one."

I kept my word. After he left I went down into the basement to look up a bug for him. I saw several of them, but couldn't catch a one. I gave up in disgust.

After supper, Arthur Belsen came popping from across the alley. He was in a dither, but that was not unusual. He is a birdlike, nervous man and it doesn't take too much to get him all upset.

"I hear that boulder in your garden is an agate," he said to me. "What do you intend to do with it?"

"Why, I don't know. Sell it, I suppose, if anyone wants to buy it."

"It might be valuable," said Belsen. "You can't just leave it out there. Someone might come along and pinch it."

"Guess there's nothing else to do," I told him. "I certainly can't move it and I'm not going to sit up all night to guard it."

"You don't need to sit up all night," said Belsen. "I can fix it for you. We can rig up a nest of trip wires and hook up an alarm."

I wasn't too impressed and tried to discourage him, but he was like a beagle on a rabbit trail. He went back to his basement and came out with a batch of wire and a kit of tools and we fell to work.

We worked until almost bedtime getting the wires rigged up and an alarm bell installed just inside the kitchen door. Helen took a sour view of it. She didn't like the idea of messing up her kitchen, agate or no agate.

In the middle of the night the clamor of the bell jerked me out of bed, wondering what all the racket was. Then I remembered and went rushing for the stairs. On the third step from the bottom I stepped on something that rolled beneath my foot and sent me pitching down the stairs into the living room. I fell sprawling and skidded into a lamp, which landed on top of me and hit me on the head. I brought up against a chair, tangled with the lamp.

A marble, I thought. That damn kid has been strewing marbles all over the house again! He's too big for that. He knows better than to leave marbles on the stairs.

16

In the bright moonlight pouring through the picture window I saw the marble and it was moving rapidly—*not rolling, moving!* And there were a lot of other marbles, racing across the floor. Sparkling golden marbles running in the moonlight.

And that wasn't all—in the center of the living room stood the refrigerator!

The alarm bell was still clanging loudly and I picked myself up and got loose from the lamp and rushed for the kitchen door. Behind me I heard Helen yelling at me from the landing.

I got the door open and went racing in bare feet through the dew-soaked grass around the corner of the house.

A puzzled dog was standing by the boulder. He had managed to get one foot caught in one of Belsen's silly wires and he was standing there, three-legged, trying to get loose.

I yelled at him and bent over, scrabbling in the grass, trying to find something I could throw at him. He made a sudden lurch and freed himself. He took off up the alley, ears flapping in the breeze.

Behind me the clanging bell fell silent.

I turned around and trailed back to the house, feeling like a fool.

I suddenly remembered that I had seen the refrigerator standing in the living room. But, I told myself, that must be wrong. The refrigerator was in the kitchen and no one would have moved it. There was, first of all, no reason for a refrigerator to be in the living room; its place was in the kitchen. No one would have wanted to move it, and even if they did, they'd have made noise enough to wake the house if they'd tried to do it.

I was imagining things, I told myself. The boulder and the bugs had got me all upset and I was seeing things.

But I wasn't.

The refrigerator still stood in the center of the living room. The plug had been pulled out of the outlet and the cord trailed across the floor. A puddle of water from the slowly-thawing box had soaked into the carpet.

"It's ruining the carpet!" Helen shrieked at me, standing in a corner and staring at the errant refrigerator. "And the food will all be spoiled and ..."

Billy came stumbling down the stairs, still half asleep.

17

"What's going on?" he asked.

"I don't know," I said.

I almost told him about the bugs I'd seen running in the house, but caught myself in time. There was no use upsetting Helen any more than she was right then.

"Let's get that box back where it belongs," I suggested, as matter-of-factly as I could. "The three of us can do it."

We tugged and shoved and hauled and lifted and got it back in its proper place and plugged it in again. Helen found some rags and started to mop up the sopping carpet.

"Was there something at the boulder, Dad?" asked Billy.

"A dog," I told him. "Nothing but a dog."

"I was against it from the start," declared Helen, on her knees, angrily mopping the carpet. "It was a lot of foolishness. No one would have stolen the boulder. It isn't something you can just pick up and carry off. That Arthur Belsen's crazy."

"I agree with you," I told her, ruefully. "But he is a conscientious sort of fellow and a determined cuss and he thinks in terms of gadgets. . . ."

"We won't get a wink of sleep," she said. "We'll be up a dozen times a night, chasing off stray dogs and cats. And I don't believe the boulder is an agate. All we have to go on is Tommy Henderson."

"Tommy is a rockhound," Billy told her, staunchly defending his pal. "He knows an agate when he sees one. He's got a big shoe box full of ones he's found."

And here we were, I thought, arguing about the boulder, when the thing that should most concern us—the happening with the most brain-twisting implications—was the refrigerator.

And a thought came to me—a floating, random thought that came bumbling out of nowhere and glanced against my mind. I shivered at the thought and it came back again and burrowed into me and I was stuck with it:

What if there was some connection between the refrigerator and the bugs?

Helen got up from the floor. "There," she said accusingly, "that is the best I can do. I hope the carpet isn't ruined."

But a bug, I told myself—no bug could move a refrigerator. No bug, nor a thousand bugs. And what was more and final, no bug would want to move one. No bug would care whether a

18

refrigerator was in the living room or kitchen.

Helen was very businesslike. She spread the wet cloth out on the sink to dry. She went into the living room and turned out the lights.

"We might as well get back to bed," she said. "If we are lucky, we can get some sleep."

I went over to the alarm beside the kitchen door and jerked the connections loose.

"Now," I told her, "we can get some sleep."

I didn't really expect to get any. I expected to stay awake the rest of the night, worrying about the refrigerator. But I did drop off, although not for very long.

At six-thirty Belsen turned on his orchestra and brought me out of bed.

Helen sat up, with her hands against her ears.

"Oh, not again!" she said.

I went around and closed the windows. It cut down the noise a little.

"Put the pillow over your head," I told her.

I dressed and went downstairs. The refrigerator was in the kitchen and everything seemed to be all right. There were a few of the bugs running around, but they weren't bothering anything.

I made myself some breakfast; then I went to work. And this was the second day running I'd gone early to the office. If this kept up, I told myself, the neighborhood would have to get together and do something about Belsen and his symphony.

Everything went all right. I sold a couple of policies during the morning and lined up a third.

When I came back to the office early in the afternoon a wild-eyed individual was awaiting me.

"You Marsden?" he demanded. "You the guy that's got an agate boulder?"

"That's what I'm told it is," I said.

The man was a little runt. He wore sloppy khaki pants and engineer boots. Stuck in his belt was a rock hammer, one of those things with a hammer on one end of the head and a pick on the other.

"I heard about it," said the man, excitedly and a bit belligerently, "and I can't believe it. There isn't any agate that ever ran that big."

19

I didn't like his attitude. "If you came here to argue ..."

"It isn't that," said the man. "My name is Christian Barr. I'm a rockhound, you understand. Been at it all my life. Have a big collection. President of our rock club. Win prizes at almost every show. And I thought if you had a rock like this ..."

"Yes?"

"Well, if you had a rock like this, I might make an offer for it. I'd have to see it first."

I jammed my hat back on my head.

"Let us go," I said.

In the garden, Barr walked entranced around the boulder. He wet his thumb and rubbed the smooth places on its hide. He leaned close and inspected it. He ran a speculative hand across its surface. He muttered to himself.

"Well?" I asked.

"It's an agate," Barr told me, breathlessly. "Apparently a single, complete agate. Look here, this sort of pebbled, freckled surface—well, that's the inverse imprint of the volcanic bubble inside of which it formed. There's the characteristic mottling on the surface one would expect to find. And the fractures where the surface has been nicked show subconchoidal cleavage. And, of course, there is the indication of some banding."

He pulled the rock hammer from his belt and idly banged the boulder. It rang like a monstrous bell.

Barr froze and his mouth dropped open.

"It hadn't ought to do that," he explained as soon as he regained some of his composure. "It sounds as if it's hollow."

He rapped it once again and the boulder pealed.

"Agate is strange stuff," he said. "It's tougher than the best of steel. I suppose you could make a bell out of it if you could only fabricate it."

He stuck the hammer back into his belt and prowled around the boulder.

"It could be a thunderegg," he said, talking to himself. "But no, it can't be that. A thunderegg has agate in its center and not on the surface. And this is banded agate and you don't find banded agate associated with a thunderegg."

"What is a thunderegg?" I asked, but he didn't answer. He had hunkered down and was examining the bottom portion.

"Marsden," he asked, "how much will you take for this?"

20

"You'd have to name a figure," I told him. "I have no idea what it's worth."

"I'll give you a thousand as it stands."

"I don't think so," I said. Not that I didn't think it was enough, but on the principle that it's never wise to take a man's first figure.

"If it weren't hollow," Barr told me, "it would be worth a whole lot more."

"You can't be sure it's hollow."

"You heard it when I rapped it."

"Maybe that's just the way it sounds."

Barr shook his head. "It's all wrong," he complained. "No banded agate ever ran this big. No agate's ever hollow. And you don't know where this one came from."

I didn't answer him. There was no reason for me to.

"Look here," he said, after a while. "There's a hole in it. Down here near the bottom."

I squatted down to look where his finger pointed. There was a neat, round hole, no more than half an inch in diameter; no haphazard hole, but round and sharply cut, as if someone might have drilled it.

Barr hunted around and found a heavy weed stalk and stripped off the leaves. The stalk, some two feet of it, slid into the hole.

Barr squatted back and stared, frowning, at the boulder.

"She's hollow, sure as hell," he said.

I didn't pay too much attention to him. I was beginning to sweat a little. For another crazy thought had come bumbling along and fastened onto me:

That hole would be just big enough for one of those bugs to get through!

"Tell you what," said Barr. "I'll raise that offer to two thousand and take it off your hands."

I shook my head. I was going off my rocker linking up the bugs and boulder—even if there was a bug-size hole drilled into the boulder. I remembered that I likewise had linked the bugs with the refrigerator—and it must be perfectly obvious to any-one that the bugs could not have anything to do with either the refrigerator or the boulder.

They were just ordinary bugs—well, maybe not just ordinary bugs, but, anyhow, just bugs. Dobby had been puzzled by them,

21

but Dobby would be the first, I knew, to tell you that there were many insects unclassified as yet. This might be a species which suddenly had flared into prominence, favored by some strange quirk of ecology, after years of keeping strictly under cover.

"You mean to say," asked Barr, astonished, "that you won't take two thousand?"

"Huh?" I asked, coming back to earth.

"I just offered you two thousand for the boulder."

I took a good hard look at him. He didn't look like the kind of man who'd spend two thousand for a hobby. More than likely, I told myself, he knew a good thing when he saw it and was out to make a killing. He wanted to snap this boulder up before I knew what it was worth.

"I'd like to think it over," I told him, warily. "If I decide to take the offer, where can I get in touch with you?"

He told me curtly and gruffly said goodbye. He was sore about my not taking his two thousand. He went stumping around the garage and a moment later I heard him start his car and drive away.

I squatted there and wondered if maybe I shouldn't have taken that two thousand. Two thousand was a lot of money and I could have used it. But the man had been too anxious and he'd had a greedy look.

Now, however, there was one thing certain. I couldn't leave the boulder out here in the garden. It was much too valuable to be left unguarded. Somehow or other I'd have to get it into the garage where I could lock it up. George Montgomery had a block and tackle and maybe I could borrow it and use it to move the boulder.

I started for the house to tell Helen the good news, although I was pretty sure she'd read me a lecture for not selling for two thousand.

She met me at the kitchen door and threw her arms around my neck and kissed me.

"Randall," she caroled, happily, "it's just too wonderful."

"I think so, too," I said, wondering how in the world she could have known about it.

"Just come and look at them," she cried. "The bugs are cleaning up the house!"

"They're what!" I yelled.

"Come and look," she urged, tugging at my arm. "Did you

22

ever see the like of it? Everything's just shining!"

I stumbled after her into the living room and stared in disbelief that bordered close on horror.

They were working in battalions and they were purposeful about it. One gang of them was going over a chair back, four rows of them in line creeping up the chair back, and it was like one of those before-and-after pictures. The lower half of the chair back was so clean it looked like new, while the upper half was dingy.

Another gang was dusting an end table and a squad of others was working on the baseboard in the corner and a small army of them was polishing up the television set.

"They've got the carpeting all done!" squealed Helen. "And this end of the room is dusted and there are some of them starting on the fireplace. I never could get Nora to even touch the fireplace. And now I won't need Nora. Randall, do you realize that these bugs will save us the twenty dollars a week that we've been paying Nora? I wonder if you'll let me have that twenty dollars for my very own. There are so many things I need. I haven't had a new dress for ages and I should have another hat and I saw the cutest pair of shoes the other day...."

"But bugs!" I yelled. "You are afraid of bugs. You detest the things. And bugs don't clean carpeting. All they do is eat it."

"These bugs are cute," protested Helen, happily, "and I'm not afraid of them. They're not like ants and spiders. They don't give you a crawly feeling. They are so clean themselves and they are so friendly and so cheerful. They are even pretty. And I just love to watch them work. Isn't it cunning, the way they get together in a bunch to work? They're just like a vacuum cleaner. They just move over something and the dust and dirt are gone."

I stood there, looking at them hard at work, and I felt an icy finger moving up my spine, for no matter how it might violate common sense, now I knew that the things I had been thinking, about the refrigerator and the boulder, had not been half as crazy as they might have seemed.

"I'm going to phone Amy," said Helen, starting for the kitchen. "This is just too wonderful to keep. Maybe we could give her some of the bugs. What do you think, Randall? Just

23

enough of them to give her house a start."

"Hey, wait a minute," I hollered at her. "These things aren't bugs."

"I don't care what they are," said Helen, airily, already dialing Amy's number, "just so they clean the house."

"But, Helen, if you'd only listen to me ..."

"Shush," she said playfully. "How can I talk to Amy if you keep— Oh, hello, Amy, is that you ...?"

I saw that it was hopeless. I retreated in complete defeat.

I went around the house to the garage, intending to move some stuff to make room for the boulder at the back.

The door was open. Inside was Billy, busy at the work bench.

"Hello, son," I said, as cheerfully as I could manage. "What's going on?"

"I'm making some bug traps, Dad. To catch some of the bugs that are cleaning up the house. Tommy's partners with me. He went home to get some bait."

"Bait?"

"Sure. We found out that they like agates."

I reached out and grabbed a studding to hold myself erect. Things were going just a bit too fast to take.

"We tried out the traps down in the basement," Billy told me. "There are a lot of the bugs down there. We tried everything for bait. We tried cheese and apples and dead flies and a lot of other things, but the bugs weren't having any. Tommy had an agate in his pocket, just a little gravel agate that he picked up. So we tried that."

"But why an agate, son? I can't think of anything less likely ..."

"Well, you see, it was this way, Dad. We tried everything. ..."

"Yes," I said, "I can see the logic of it."

"Trouble is," Billy went on, "we have to use plastic for the traps. It's the only thing that will hold the bugs. They burst right out of a trap made of anything but plastic."

"Now, just a minute there," I warned him. "Once you catch these bugs, what do you intend to do with them?"

"Sell them, naturally," said Billy. "Tommy and me figured everyone would want them. Once the people around here find out how they'll clean a house, everyone will want them. We'll charge five dollars for half a dozen of them. That's a whole lot cheaper than a vacuum cleaner."

"But just six bugs ..."

"They multiply," said Billy. "They must multiply real fast. A day or two ago we had just a few of them and now the house is swarming."

Billy went on working on the trap.

Finally he said, "Maybe, Dad, you'd like to come in with us on the deal? We need some capital. We have to buy some plastic to make more and better traps. We might be able to make a big thing out of it."

"Look, son. Have you sold any of the bugs?"

"Well, we tried to, but no one would believe us. So we thought we'd wait until Mom noised it around a bit."

"What did you do with the bugs you caught?"

"We took them over to Dr. Wells. I remembered that he wanted some. We gave them to him free."

"Billy, I wish you'd do something for me."

"Sure, Dad. What is it?"

"Don't sell any of the bugs. Not right away at least. Not until I say that it's okay."

"But, gee, Dad ..."

"Son, I have a hunch. I think the bugs are alien."

"Me and Tommy figured that they might be."

"You what!"

"It was this way, Dad. At first we figured we'd sell them just as curiosities. That was before we knew how they would clean a house. We thought some folks might want them because they looked so different, and we tried to figure out a sales pitch. And Tommy said why don't we call them alien bugs, like the bugs from Mars or something. And that started us to thinking and the more we thought about it the more we thought they might really be bugs from Mars. They aren't insects, nor anything else so far as we could find. They're not like anything on Earth. . . ."

"All right," I said. "All right!"

That's the way kids are these days. You can't keep up with them. You think you have something all nailed down and neat and here they've beat you to it. It happens all the time.

I tell you, honestly, it does nothing for a man.

"I suppose," I said, "that while you were figuring all this

out, you also got it doped how they might have got here."

"We can't be really sure," said Billy, "but we have a theory. That boulder out in back—we found a hole in it just the right size for these bugs. So we sort of thought they used that."

"You won't believe me, son," I told him, "but I was thinking the same thing. But the part that's got me stumped is what they used for power. What made the boulder move through space?"

"Well, gee, Dad, we don't know that. But there is something else. They could have used the boulder for their food all the time they traveled. There'd be just a few of them, most likely, and they'd get inside the boulder and there'd be all that food, maybe enough of it to last them years and years. So they'd eat the agate, hollowing out the boulder and making it lighter so it could travel faster—well, if not faster, at least a little easier. But they'd be very careful not to chew any holes in it until they'd landed and it was time to leave."

"But agate is just rock. . . ."

"You weren't listening, Dad," said Billy, patiently. "I told you that agate was the only bait they'd go for."

"Randall," said Helen, coming down the driveway, "if you don't mind, I'd like to use the car to go over and see Amy. She wants me to tell her all about the bugs."

"Go ahead," I said. "Any way you look at it, my day is shot. I may as well stay home."

She went tripping back down the driveway and I said to Billy: "You just lay off everything until I get back."

"Where are you going, Dad?"

"Over to see Dobby."

I found Dobby roosting on a bench beneath an apple tree, his face all screwed up with worry. But it didn't stop him from talking.

"Randall," he said, beginning to talk as soon as I hove in sight, "this is a sad day for me. All my life I've been vastly proud of my professional exactitude in my chosen calling. But this day I violated, willingly and knowingly and in a fit of temper, every precept of experimental observation and laboratory technique."

"That's too bad," I said, wondering what he was talking about. Which was not unusual. One often had to wonder what he was getting at.

"It's those damn bugs of yours," Dobby accused me explosively.

"But you said you wanted some more bugs. Billy remembered that and he brought some over."

"And so I did. I wanted to carry forward my examination of them. I wanted to dissect one and see what made him go. Perhaps you recall my telling you about the hardness of the exoskeletons."

"Yes, of course I do."

"Randall," said Dobby sadly, "would you believe me if I told you that exoskeleton was so hard I could do nothing with it? I couldn't cut it and I couldn't peel it off. So you know what I did?"

"I have no idea," I declared, somewhat exasperated. I hoped that he'd soon get to the point, but there was no use in hurrying him. He always took his time.

"Well, I'll tell you, then," said Dobby, seething. "I took one of those little so-and-sos and I put him on an anvil. Then I picked up a hammer and I let him have it. And I tell you frankly that I am not proud of it. It constituted, in every respect, a most improper laboratory technique."

"I wouldn't let that worry me at all," I told him. "You'll simply have to put this down as an unusual circumstance. The important thing, it seems to me, is what you learned about the bug...."

And then I had a terrible thought. "Don't tell me the hammer failed!"

"Not at all," said Dobby with some satisfaction. "It did a job on him. He was smashed to smithereens."

I sat down on the bench beside him and settled down to wait. I knew that in due time he'd tell me.

"An amazing thing," said Dobby. "Yes, a most amazing thing. That bug was made of crystals—of something that looked like the finest quartz. There was no protoplasm in him. Or, at least," he qualified, judiciously, "none I could detect."

"But a crystal bug! That's impossible!"

"Impossible," said Dobby. "Yes, of course, by any earthly standard. It runs counter to everything we've ever known or thought. But the question rises: Can our earthly standards, even remotely, be universal?"

I sat there, without saying anything, but somehow I felt a

27

great relief that someone else was thinking the same thing I had thought. It went to prove, just slightly, that I wasn't crazy.

"Of course," said Dobby, "it had to happen sometime. Soon or late, it should be almost inevitable that some alien intelligence would finally seek us out. And knowing this, we speculated on monsters and monstrosities, but we fell short of the actual mark of horr—"

"There's no reason at the moment," I told him, hastily, "that we should fear the bugs. They might, in fact, become a useful ally. Even now they are cooperating. They seemed to strike up some sort of deal. We furnish them a place to live and they, in turn ..."

"You're mistaken, Randall," Dobby warned me solemnly. "These things are alien beings. Don't imagine for a moment that they and the human race might have a common purpose or a single common concept. Their life process, whatever it may be, is entirely alien to us. So must be their viewpoints. A spider is blood-brother to you as compared with these."

"But we had ants and wasps and they cleaned out the ants and wasps."

"They may have cleaned out the ants and wasps, but it was no part, I am sure, of a cooperative effort. It was no attempt on their part to butter up the human in whose dwelling place they happened to take refuge, or set up their camp, or carve out their beachhead, however you may put it. I have grave doubts that they are aware of you at all except as some mysterious and rather shadowy monstrosity they can't bother with as yet. Sure they killed your insects, but in this they did no more than operate on a level common with their own existence. The insects might have been in their way or they may have recognized in them some potential threat or hindrance."

"But even so, we can use them," I told him impatiently, "to control our insect pests, or carriers of disease."

"Can we?" Dobby asked. "What makes you think we can? And it would not be insect pests alone, but rather all insects. Would you, then, deprive our plant life of its pollination agents—to mention just one example of thousands?"

"You may be right," I said, "but you can't tell me that we must be afraid of bugs, of even crystal bugs. Even if they should turn out to be a menace, we could find a way in which to cope with them."

28

"I have been sitting here and thinking, trying to get it straight within my mind," said Dobby, "and one thing that has occurred to me is that here we may be dealing with a social concept we've never met with on this planet. I'm convinced that these aliens must necessarily operate on the hive-mind principle. We face not one of them alone nor the total number of them, but we face the sum total of them as a single unit, as a single mind and a single expression of purpose and performance."

"If you really think they're dangerous, what would you have us do?"

"I still have my anvil and my hammer."

"Cut out the kidding, Dobby."

"You are right," said Dobby. "This is no joking matter, nor is it one for an anvil and a hammer. My best suggestion is that the area be evacuated and an atom bomb be dropped."

Billy came tearing down the path.

"Dad!" he was yelling. "Dad!"

"Hold up there," I said, clutching at his arm. "What is going on?"

"Someone is ripping up our furniture," yelled Billy, "and then throwing it outdoors."

"Now, wait a minute—are you sure?"

"I saw them doing it," yelled Billy. "Gosh, will Mom be sore!"

I didn't wait to hear any more. I started for the house as fast as I could go. Billy followed close behind me and Dobby brought up the rear, white whiskers bristling like an excited billy goat.

The screen door off the kitchen was standing open as if someone had propped it, and outside, beyond the stoop, lay a pile of twisted fabric and the odds and ends of dismembered chairs.

I went up the steps in one bound and headed for the door. And just as I reached the doorway I saw this great mass of stuff bulleting straight toward me and I ducked aside. A limp and gutted love seat came hurtling out the door and landed on the pile of debris. It sagged into a grotesque resemblance of its former self.

By this time I was good and sore. I dived for the pile and grabbed up a chair leg. I got a good grip on it and rushed

29

through the door and across the kitchen into the living room. I had the club at ready and if there'd been anybody there I would have let him have it.

But there was no one there—no one I could see.

The refrigerator was back in the center of the room and heaped all about it were piles of pots and pans. The tangled coil springs from the love seat were leaning crazily against it and scattered all about the carpeting there were nuts and bolts, washers, brads and nails and varying lengths of wire.

There was a strange creaking noise from somewhere and I glanced hurriedly around to find out what it was. I found out, all right.

Over on one corner, my favorite chair was slowly and deliberately and weirdly coming apart. The upholstery nails were rising smoothly from the edging of the fabric—rising from the wood as if by their own accord—and dropping to the floor with tiny patterings. As I watched, a bolt fell to the floor and one leg bent underneath the chair and the chair tipped over. The upholstery nails kept right on coming out.

And as I stood there watching this, I felt the anger draining out of me and a fear come dribbling in to take its place. I started to get cold all over and I could feel the gooseflesh rising.

I started sneaking out. I didn't dare to turn my back, so I backed carefully away and I kept my club ready.

I bumped into something and let out a whoop and spun around and raised my club to strike.

It was Dobby. I just stopped the club in time.

"Randall," said Dobby calmly, "it's those bugs of yours again."

He gestured toward the ceiling and I looked. The ceiling was a solid mass of golden-gleaming bugs.

I lost some of my fear at seeing them and started to get sore again. I pulled back my arm and aimed the club up at the ceiling. I was ready to let the little stinkers have it, when Dobby grabbed my arm.

"Don't go getting them stirred up," he yelled. "No telling what they'd do."

I tried to jerk my arm away from him, but he hung on to it.

"It is my considered opinion," he declared, even as he

30

wrestled with me, "that the situation has evolved beyond the point where it can be handled by the private citizen."

I gave up. It was undignified trying to get my arm loose from Dobby's clutching paws and I likewise began to see that a club was no proper weapon to use against the bugs.

"You may be right," I said.

I saw that Billy was peering through the door.

"Get out of here," I yelled at him. "You're in the line of fire. They'll be throwing that chair out of here in another minute. They're almost through with it."

Billy ducked back out of sight.

I walked out to the kitchen and hunted through a cupboard drawer until I found the phone book. I looked up the number and dialed the police.

"This is Sergeant Andrews talking," said a voice.

"Now, listen closely, Sergeant," I said, "I have some bugs out here...."

"Ain't we all?" the sergeant asked in a happy tone of voice.

"Sergeant," I told him, trying to sound as reasonable as I could, "I know that this sounds funny. But these are a different kind of bug. They're breaking up my furniture and throwing it outdoors."

"I tell you what," the sergeant said, still happy. "You better go on back to bed and try to sleep it off. If you don't, I'll have to run you in."

"Sergeant," I told him, "I am completely sober ..."

A hollow click came from the other end and the phone went dead.

I dialed the number back.

"Sergeant Andrews," said the voice.

"You just hung up on me," I yelled. "What do you mean by that? I'm a sober, law-abiding, taxpaying citizen and I'm entitled to protection, and even if you don't think so, to some courtesy as well. And when I tell you I have bugs ..."

"All right," said the sergeant wearily. "Since you are asking for it. What's your name and address?"

I gave them to him.

"And Mr. Marsden," said the sergeant.

"What is it now?"

"You better have those bugs. If you know what's good for you, there better be some bugs."

31

I slammed down the phone and turned around.

Dobby came tearing out of the living room.

"Look out! Here it comes!" he yelled.

My favorite chair, what was left of it, came swishing through the air. It hit the door and stuck. It jiggled violently and broke loose to drop on the pile outside.

"Amazing," Dobby panted. "Truly amazing. But it explains a lot."

"Tell me," I snapped at him, "what explains a lot?"

I was getting tired of Dobby's ramblings.

"Telekinesis," said Dobby.

"Tele-what?"

"Well, maybe only teleportation," Dobby admitted sheepishly. "That's the ability to move things by the power of mind alone."

"And you think this teleportation business bears out your hive-mind theory?"

Dobby looked at me with some astonishment. "That's exactly what I meant," he said.

"What I can't figure out," I told him, "is why they're doing this."

"Of course you can't," said Dobby. "No one expects you to. No one can presume to understand an alien motive. On the surface of it, it would appear they are collecting metal, and that well may be exactly what they're doing. But the mere fact of their metal grabbing does not go nearly far enough. To truly understand their motive ..."

A siren came screaming down the street.

"There they are," I said, racing for the door.

The police car pulled up to the curb and two officers vaulted out.

"You Marsden?" asked the first one.

I told him that I was.

"That's funny," said the second one. "Sarge said he was stinko."

"Say," said the first one, staring at the pile of wreckage outside the kitchen door, "what is going on here?"

Two chair legs came whistling out the door and thudded to the ground.

"Who is in there throwing out the stuff?" the second cop demanded.

"Just the bugs," I told them. "Just the bugs and Dobby. I guess Dobby's still in there."

"Let's go in and grab this Dobby character," said the first one, "before he wrecks the joint."

I stayed behind. There was no use of going in. All they'd do would be ask a lot of silly questions and there were enough of them I could ask myself without listening to the ones thought up by someone else.

A small crowd was beginning to gather. Billy had rounded up some of his pals and neighbor women were rushing from house to house, cackling like excited chickens. Several cars had stopped and their occupants sat gawping.

I walked out to the street and sat down on the curbing.

And now, I thought, it all had become just a little clearer. If Dobby was right about this teleportation business, and the evidence said he was, then the boulder could have been the ship the bugs had used to make their way to Earth. If they could use their power to tear up furniture and throw it out of the house, they could use that selfsame power to move anything through space. It needn't have been the boulder; it could have been anything at all.

Billy, in his uninhibited, boyish thinking, probably had struck close to the truth—they had used the boulder because it was their food.

The policemen came pounding back out of the house and stopped beside me.

"Say, mister," said one of them, "do you have the least idea what is going on?"

I shook my head. "You better talk to Dobby. He's the one with answers."

"He says these things are from Mars."

"Not Mars," said the second officer. "It was you who said it might be Mars. He said from the stars."

"He's a funny-talking old coot," complained the first policeman. "A lot of stuff he says is more than a man can swallow."

"Jake," said the other one, "we better start doing something about this crowd. We can't let them get too close."

"I'll radio for help," said Jake.

He went to the police car and climbed into it.

"You stick around," the other said to me.

"I'm not going anywhere," I said.

33

The crowd was good-sized by now. More cars had stopped and some of the people in them had gotten out, but most of them just sat and stared. There were an awful lot of kids by this time and the women were still coming, perhaps from blocks away. Word spreads fast in an area like ours.

Dobby came ambling down the yard. He sat down beside me and started pawing at his whiskers.

"It makes no sense," he said, "but, then, of course, it wouldn't."

"What I can't figure out," I told him, "is why they cleaned the house. Why did it have to be spic and span before they started piling up the metal? There must be a reason for it."

A car screeched down the street and slammed up to the curb just short of where we sat. Helen came bustling out of it.

"I can't turn my back a minute," she declared, "but something up and happens."

"It's your bugs," I said. "Your nice house-cleaning bugs. They're ripping up the place."

"Why don't you stop them, then?"

"Because I don't know how."

"They're aliens,' Dobby told her calmly. "They came from somewhere out in space."

"Dobby Wells, you keep out of this! You've caused me all the trouble I can stand. The idea of getting Billy interested in insects! He's had the place cluttered up all summer."

A man came rushing up. He squatted down beside me and started pawing at my arm. I turned around and saw that it was Barr, the rockhound.

"Marsden," he said, excitedly, "I have changed my mind. I'll give you five thousand for that boulder. I'll write you out a check right now."

"What boulder?" Helen asked. "You mean our boulder out in the back?"

"That's the one," said Barr. "I've got to have that boulder."

"Sell it to him," Helen said.

"I will not," I told her.

"Randall Marsden," she screamed, "you can't turn down five thousand! Think of what five thousand ..."

"I can turn it down," I told her, firmly. "It's worth a whole lot more than that. It's not just an agate boulder any longer.

It's the first spaceship that ever came to Earth. I can get anything I ask."

Helen gasped.

"Dobby," she asked weakly, "is he telling me the truth?"

"I think," said Dobby, "that for once he is."

We got up to start across the street.

"Lady," said the officer, "you'll have to move your car."

"You folks will have to get across the street," he said. "As soon as the others get here, we'll cordon off the place."

We got up to start across the street.

"Lady," said the officer, "you'll have to move your car."

"If you two want to stay together," Dobby offered, "I'll drive it down the street."

Helen gave him the keys and the two of us walked across the street. Dobby got into the car and drove off.

The officers were hustling the other cars away.

A dozen police cars arrived. Men piled out of them. They started pushing back the crowd. Others fanned out to start forming a circle around the house.

Broken furniture, bedding, clothing, draperies from time to time came flying out the kitchen door. The pile of debris grew bigger by the moment.

We stood across the street and watched our house be wrecked.

"They must be almost through by now," I said, with a strange detachment. "I wonder what comes next."

"Randall," said Helen tearfully, clinging to my arm, "what do we do now? They're wrecking all my things. How about it—is it covered by insurance?"

"Why, I don't know," I said. "I never thought of it."

And that was the truth of it—it hadn't crossed my mind. And me an insurance man!

I had written that policy myself and now I tried desperately to remember what the fine print might have said and I had a sinking feeling. How, I asked myself, could anything like this be covered? It certainly was no hazard that could have been anticipated.

"Anyhow," I said, "we still have the boulder. We can sell the boulder."

"I still think we should have taken the five thousand," Helen

35

told me. "What if the Government should move in and just grab the boulder off?"

And she was right, I told myself. This would be just the sort of thing in which the Government could become intensely interested.

I began to think myself that maybe we should have taken that five thousand.

Three policemen walked across the yard and went into the house. Almost at once they came tearing out again. Pouring out behind them came a swarm of glittering dots that hummed and buzzed and swooped so fast they seemed to leave streaks of their golden glitter in the air behind them. The policemen ran in weaving fashion, ducking and dodging. They waved their hands in the air above their heads.

The crowd surged back and began to run. The police cordon broke and retreated with what dignity it could.

I found myself behind the house across the street, my hand still gripping Helen's arm. She was madder than a hornet.

"You needn't have pulled me along so fast," she told me. "I could have made it by myself. You made me lose my shoes."

"Forget your shoes," I told her sharply. "This thing is getting serious. You go and round up Billy and the two of you get out of here. Go up to Amy's place."

"Do you know where Billy is?"

"He's around somewhere. He is with his pals. Just look for a bunch of boys."

"And you?"

"I'll be along," I said.

"You'll be careful, Randall?"

I patted her shoulder and stooped down to kiss her. "I'll be careful. I'm not very brave, you know. Now go and get the boy."

She started away and then turned back. "Will we ever go back home?" she asked.

"I think we will," I said, "and soon. Someone will find a way to get them out of there."

I watched her walk away and felt the chilly coldness of the kindness of my lie.

Would we, in solemn truth, ever go back home again? Would the entire world, all of humanity, ever be at home again? Would the golden bugs take away the smug comfort and the warm security that Man had known for ages in his sole possession of a planet of his own?

I went up the backyard slope and found Helen's shoes. I put them in my pocket. I came to the back of the house and peeked around the corner.

The bugs had given up the chase, but now a squadron of them flew in a lazy, shining circle around and just above the house. It was plain to see that they were on patrol.

I ducked back around the house and sat down in the grass, with my back against the house. It was a warm and blue-sky summer day; the kind of day a man should mow his lawn.

A slobbering horror, I thought, no matter how obscene or fearful, might be understood, might be fought against. But the cold assuredness with which the golden bugs were directed to their purpose, the self-centered, vicious efficiency with which they operated, was something else again.

And their impersonal detachment, their very disregard of us, was like a chilly blast upon human dignity.

I heard footsteps and looked up, startled.

It was Arthur Belsen and he was upset.

But that was not unusual. Belsen could get upset at something that was downright trivial.

"I was looking for you everywhere," he chattered. "I met Dobby just a while ago and he tells me these bugs of yours ..."

"They're no bugs of mine," I told him sharply. I was getting tired of everyone talking as if I owned the bugs, as if I might be somehow responsible for their having come to Earth.

"Well, anyway, he was telling me they are after metal."

I nodded. "That's what they're after. Maybe it's precious stuff to them. Maybe they haven't got too much of it wherever they are from."

And I thought about the agate boulder. If they had had metal, certainly they'd not have used the agate boulder.

"I had an awful time getting home," said Belsen. "I thought there was a fire. There are cars parked in the street for blocks and an awful crowd. I was lucky to get through."

"Come on and sit down," I told him. "Stop your fidgeting."

But he paid no attention to me.

"I have an awful lot of metal," he said. "All those machines of mine down in the basement. I've put a lot of time and work

37

and money into those machines and I can't let anything happen to them. You don't think the bugs will start branching out, do you?"

"Branching out?"

"Well, yes, you know—after they get through with everything in your house, they might start getting into other houses."

"I hadn't thought of it," I said. "I suppose that it could happen."

I sat there and thought about it and I had visions of them advancing house by house, cleaning out and salvaging all the metal, putting it into one big pile until it covered the entire block and eventually the city.

"Dobby says that they are crystal. Isn't that a funny thing for bugs to be?"

I said nothing. After all, he was talking to himself.

"But crystal can't be alive," protested Belsen. "Crystal is stuff that things are made of. Vacuum tubes and such. There is no life in it."

"Don't try to fight with me," I told him. "I can't help it if they are crystal."

There seemed to be a lot of ruckus going on out in the street and I got on my feet to peer around the corner of the house.

For a moment there was nothing to see. Everything looked peaceful. One or two policemen were running around excitedly, but I couldn't see that anything was happening. It looked just as it had before.

Then a door slowly, almost majestically, detached itself from one of the police cars parked along the curb and started floating toward the open kitchen door. It reached the door and made a neat left turn and disappeared inside.

A rear vision mirror sailed flashing through the air. It was followed by a siren. Both disappeared within the house.

Good Lord, I told myself, the bugs are going after the cars!

Now I saw that a couple of the cars were already minus hoods and fenders and that some other doors were missing.

The bugs, I thought, had finally really hit the jackpot. They wouldn't stop until they'd stripped the cars clean down to the tires.

And I was thinking, too, with a strange perverse reaction,

that there wasn't nearly room enough inside the house to pack all those dismantled cars. What, I wondered, would the bugs do when the house was full?

A half dozen policemen dashed across the street and started for the house. They reached the lawn before the bug patrol above the house became aware of them and swooped down in a screaming, golden arc.

The policemen ran back pell mell. The bug patrol, it's duty done, returned to circling the house. Fenders, doors, tail-lights, headlights, radio antennae, and other parts of cars continued to pour into the house.

A dog came trotting out of nowhere and went across the lawn, tail wagging in friendly curiosity.

A flight of bugs left the patrol and headed down toward him.

The dog, startled by the whistle of the diving bugs, wheeled about to run.

He was too late.

There was a sickening thud of missiles hitting flesh. The dog leaped high into the air and fell over on his back.

The bugs swooped up into the air again. There were no gaps in their ranks.

The dog lay twitching in the yard and blood ran in the grass.

I ducked back around the corner, sick. I doubled up, retching, trying hard to keep from throwing up.

I fought it off and my stomach quieted down. I peeked around the corner of the house.

All was peaceful once again. The dead dog lay sprawling in the yard. The bugs were busy with their stripping of the cars. No policemen were in sight. There was no one in sight at all. Even Belsen had disappeared somewhere.

It was different now, I told myself. The dog had made it different.

The bugs were no longer only a mystery; now they were a deadly danger. Each of them was a rifle bullet with intelligence.

I remembered something that Dobby had said just an hour or so ago. Evacuate the area, he had said, then drop an atom bomb.

And would it come to that? I wondered. Was that the measure of the danger?

No one, of course, was thinking that way yet, but in time they might. This was just the start of it. Today the city was alerted and the police were on the scene; tomorrow it might be the governor sending in some troops. And in time it would be the Federal Government. And after that, Dobby's solution might be the only answer.

The bugs hadn't spread too far as yet. But Belsen's fear was valid; in time they would expand, pushing out their beachhead block by block as there were more and more of them. For Billy had been right when he had said they must multiply real fast.

I tried to imagine how the bugs could multiply, but I had no idea.

First of all, of course, the Government would probably try to make contact with them, would attempt to achieve some communication with them—not with the creatures themselves, perhaps, but rather with that mass mind which Dobby had figured them to have.

But was it possible to communicate with creatures such as these? On what intellectual level might one approach them? And what good could possibly come of such communication if it was established? Where was the basis for understanding between these creatures and the human race?

And I realized, even as I thought all this, that I was thinking with pure panic. To approach a problem such as the bugs presented, there was need of pure objectivity—there could be no question of either fear or anger. The time had come for Man to discard the pettiness of one-planet thinking.

It was no problem of mine, of course, but thinking of it, I saw a deadly danger—that the eventual authority, whoever that might be, might delay too long in its objectivity.

There had to be a way to stop the bugs; there must be some measure to control them. Before we tried to establish contact, there must be a way in which we could contain them.

And I thought of something—of Billy telling me that to hold them once you caught them you needed a plastic trap.

I wondered briefly how the kid had known that. Perhaps it had been no more than simple trial and error. After all, he and Tommy Henderson must have tried several different kinds of traps.

Plastic might be the answer to the problem I had posed. It could be the answer if we acted before they spread too far.

And why plastic? I wondered. What element within plastic would stop them cold and hold them once they were trapped within it? Some factor, perhaps, that we would learn only after long and careful study. But it was something that did not matter now; it was enough we knew that plastic did the trick.

I stood there for a time, turning the matter in my mind, wondering who to go to.

I could go to the police, of course, but I had a feeling I would get little hearing there. The same would be true of the officials of the city. For while it was possible they might listen, they'd have to talk it over, they'd have to call a conference, they'd feel compelled to consult some expert before they did anything about it. And the Government in Washington, at the moment, was unthinkable.

The trouble was that no one was scared enough as yet. To act as quickly as they should they'd have to be scared silly—and I had had a longer time to get scared silly than any of the rest.

Then I thought of another man who was as scared as I was.

Belsen.

Belsen was the man to help me. Belsen was scared stiff.

He was an engineer and possibly he could tell me if what I had been thinking was any good or not. He could sit down and figure how it might be done. He'd know where to get the plastic that we needed and the best type of it to use and more than likely he'd know how to go about arranging for its fabrication. And he might, as well, know someone it would do some good to talk to.

I went back to the corner of the house and had a look around.

There were a few policemen in sight, but not too many of them. They weren't doing anything, just standing there and watching while the bugs kept on working at the cars. They had the bodies pretty well stripped down by now and were working on the engines. As I watched I saw one motor rise and sail toward the house. It was dripping oil, and chunks of caked grease and dust were falling off of it. I shivered at the thought of what a mess like that would do to Helen's carpeting and the decorating.

There were a few knots of spectators here and there, but all

41

of them were standing at quite a distance off.

It looked to me as if I'd have no trouble reaching Belsen's house if I circled around the block, so I started out.

I wondered if Belsen would be at home and was afraid he might not be. Most of the houses in the neighborhood seemed to be deserted. But it was a chance, I knew, that I had to take. If he wasn't at his house, I'd have to hunt him down.

I reached his place and went up the steps and rang the bell. There wasn't any answer, so I walked straight in.

The house seemed to be deserted.

"Belsen," I called.

He didn't answer me and I called again.

Then I heard footsteps clattering up a stairs.

The basement door came open and Belsen stuck his head out.

"Oh, it's you," he said. "I'm glad you came. I will need some help. I sent the family off."

"Belsen," I said, "I know what we can do. We can get a monstrous sheet of plastic and drop it on the house. That way they can't get out. Maybe we can get some helicopters, maybe four of them, one for each corner of the sheet ..."

"Come downstairs," said Belsen. "There's work for both of us."

I followed him downstairs into his workroom.

The place was orderly, as one might expect from a fuss-budget such as Belsen.

The music machines stood in straight and shining lines, the work bench was immaculate and the tools were all in place. The tape machine stood in one corner and it was all lit up like a Christmas tree.

A table stood in front of the tape machine, but it was far from tidy. It was strewn with books, some of them lying flat and open and others piled haphazardly. There were scribbled sheets of paper scattered everywhere and balled-up bunches of it lay about the floor.

"I cannot be mistaken," Belsen told me, jittery as ever. "I must be sure the first time. There'll be no second chance. I had a devil of a time getting it all figured out, but I think I have it now."

"Look, Belsen," I said, with some irritation, "I don't know what harebrained scheme you may be working on, but whatever it may be, this deal of mine is immediate and important."

"Later," Belsen told me, almost hopping up and down in his anxiety. "Later you can tell me. I have a tape I have to finish. I have the mathematics all worked out ..."

"But this is about the bugs!"

Belsen shouted at me: "And so is this, you fool! What else did you expect to find me working on? You know I can't take a chance of their getting in here. I won't let them take all this stuff I've built."

"But, Belsen ..."

"See that machine," he said, pointing to one of the smaller ones. "That's the one we'll have to use. It is battery powered. See if you can get it moved over to the door."

He swung around and scurried over to the tape machine and sat down in front of it. He began punching slowly and carefully on the keyboard and the machine began to mutter and to chuckle at him and its lights winked on and off.

I saw there was no sense in trying to talk to him until he had this business done. And there was a chance, of course, that he knew what he was doing—that he had figured out some way either to protect these machines of his or to stop the bugs.

I walked over to the machine and it was heavier than it looked. I started tugging at it and I could move it only a few inches at a time, but I kept on tugging it.

And suddenly, as I tugged away, I knew without a question what Belsen must be planning.

And I wondered why I hadn't thought of it myself, why Dobby, with all his talk of A-bombs, hadn't thought of it. But, of course, it would take a man like Belsen, with his particular hobby, to have thought of it.

The idea was so old, so ancient, so much a part of the magic past that it was almost laughable—and yet it ought to work.

Belsen got up from the machine and lifted a reel of tape from a cylinder in its side. He hurried over to me and knelt down beside the machine I'd tugged almost to the door.

"I can't be sure of exactly what they are," he told me. "Crystal. Sure, I know they're crystalline in form, but what kind of crystals—just what type of crystals? So I had to work out a sort of sliding shotgun pattern of supersonic frequencies. Somewhere in there, I hope, is the one that will synchronize with whatever structure they may have."

43

He opened a section of the small machine and started threading in the tape.

"Like the violin that broke the goblet," I said.

He grinned at me nervously. "The classical example. I see you've heard of it."

"Everyone has," I said.

"Now listen to me carefully," said Belsen. "All we have to do is flip this switch and the tape starts moving. This dial controls the volume and it's set at maximum. We'll open up the door and we'll grab the machine, one on each side of it, and we'll carry it as far as we can before we set it down. I want to get it close."

"Not too close," I cautioned. "The bugs just killed a dog. Couple of them hit him and went through him without stopping. They're animated bullets."

Belsen licked his lips. "I figured something like that."

He reached out for the door.

"Just a minute, Belsen. Have we got a right to?"

"A right to what?" he asked.

"A right to kill these things. They're the first aliens to come to visit us. There's a lot we might learn from them if we could only talk to them...."

"Talk to them?"

"Well, communicate. Get to understand them."

And I wondered what was wrong with me, that I should be talking that way.

"After what they did to the dog? After what they did to you?"

"Yes, I think," I said, "even after what they did to me."

"You're crazy," Belsen screamed.

He pulled the door wide open.

"Now!" he shouted at me.

I hesitated for a second, then grabbed hold.

The machine was heavy, but we lifted it and rushed out into the yard. We went staggering with it almost to the alley and there the momentum of our rush played out and we set it down.

I looked up toward my house and the bug patrol was there, circling at rooftop height, a flashing golden circle in the light of the setting sun.

"Maybe," Belsen panted, "maybe we can get it closer."

I bent to pick it up again and even as I did I saw the patrolling circle break.

"Look out!" I screamed. The bugs were diving at us.

"The switch!" I yelled. "The switch!"

But Belsen stood there, staring at them, frozen, speechless, stiff.

I flung myself at the machine and found the switch and flipped it and then I was groveling in the dirt, rooting into it, trying to make myself extremely thin and small.

There was no sound and, of course, I had known there would be none, but that didn't stop me from wondering why I didn't hear it. Maybe, I thought, the tape had broken; maybe the machine had failed to work.

Out of the tail of my eye I saw the patrol arrowing down on us and they seemed to hang there in the air, as if something might have stopped them, but I knew that was wrong, that it was simply fright playing tricks with time.

And I was scared, all right, but not as scared as Belsen. He still stood there, upright, unable to move a muscle, staring at oncoming death in an attitude of stricken disbelief.

They were almost on top of us. They were so close that I could see each of them as a dancing golden mote and then suddenly each little mote became a puff of shining dust and the swarm was gone.

I climbed slowly to my feet and brushed off my front.

"Snap out of it," I said to Belsen. I shook him.

He slowly turned toward me and I could see the tension going from his face.

"It worked," he said, in a flat sort of voice. "I was pretty sure it would."

"I noticed that," I said. "You're the hero of the hour."

And I said it bitterly, without even knowing why.

I left him standing there and walked slowly across the alley.

We had done it, I told myself. Right or wrong, we'd done it. The first things from space had come and we had smashed them flat.

And was this, I wondered, what would happen to us, too, when we ventured to the stars? Would we find as little patience and as little understanding? Would we act as arrogantly as these golden bugs had acted?

Would there always be the Belsens to outshout the Marsdens? Would the Marsdens always be unable or unwilling to stand up before the panic-shouting—always fearful that their attitude, slowly forming, might be antisocial? Would the driving sense of fear and the unwillingness to understand bar all things from the stars?

And that, I told myself, was a funny thing for me, of all people, to be thinking. For mine was the house the bugs had ruined.

Although, come to think of it, they might have cost me not a dime. They might have made me money. I still had the agate boulder and that was worth a fortune.

I looked quickly towards the garden and the boulder wasn't there!

I broke into a run, breath sobbing in my throat.

I stopped at the garden's edge and stared in consternation at the neat pile of shining sand.

There was one thing I'd forgotten: that an agate, as well as bugs and goblet, was also crystalline!

I turned around and stared back across the yard and I was sore clean through.

That Belsen, I thought—him and his sliding shotgun pattern!

I would take one of those machines of his and cram it down his throat!

Then I stopped dead still. There was, I realized, nothing I could do or say. Belsen was the hero, exactly as I said he was.

He was the man, alone, who'd quashed the menace from the stars.

That was what the headlines would be saying, that was what the entire world would think. Except, perhaps, a few scientists and others of their kind who didn't really count.

Belsen was the hero and if I laid a finger to him I'd probably be lynched.

And I was right. Belsen *is* the hero.

He turns on his orchestra at six o'clock each morning and there's no one in the neighborhood who'll say a word to him.

Is there anyone who knows how much it costs to sound-proof an entire house?

46

LEG. FORST.

When it was time for the postman to have come and gone, old Clyde Packer quit working on his stamps and went into the bathroom to comb his snow-white hair and beard. It was an everlasting bother, but there was no way out of it. He'd be sure to meet some of his neighbors going down and coming back and they were a snoopy lot. He felt sure that they talked about him; not that he cared, of course. And the Widow Foshay, just across the hall, was the worst one of them all.

Before going out, he opened a drawer in the big desk in the middle of the cluttered living room, upon the top of which was piled an indescribable array of litter, and found the tiny box from Unuk al Hay. From the box he took a pinch of leaf and tucked it in his cheek.

He stood for a moment, with the drawer still open, and savored the flavorful satisfaction of the taste within his mouth —not quite like peppermint, nor like whiskey, either, but with some taste akin to both and with some other tang that belonged entirely to itself. It was nothing like another man had ever tasted and he suspected that it might be habit-forming, although PugAlNash had never informed him that it was.

Perhaps, he told himself, even if Pug should so try to inform him, he could not make it out, for the Unukian's idea of how Earth's language should be written, and the grammar thereof, was a wonder to behold and could only be believed by someone who had tried to decipher one of his flowery little notes.

The box, he saw, was nearly empty, and he hoped that the queer, faithful, almost wistful little correspondent would not fail him now. But there was, he told himself, no reason to believe he would; PugAlNash, in a dozen years, had not failed him yet. Regularly another tiny box of leaf arrived when the last one was quite finished, accompanied by a friendly note— and all franked with the newest stamps from Unuk.

Never a day too soon, nor a day too late, but exactly on the dot when the last of the leaf was finished. As if PugAlNash might know, by some form of intelligence quite unknown to

47

Earth, when his friend on Earth ran out of the leaf.

A solid sort, Clyde Packer told himself. Not humanoid, naturally, but a very solid sort.

And he wondered once again what Pug might actually be like. He always had thought of him as little, but he had no idea, of course, whether he was small or large or what form his body took. Unuk was one of those planets where it was impossible for an Earthman to go, and contact and commerce with the planet had been accomplished, as was the case on so many other worlds, by an intermediary people.

And he wondered, too, what Pug did with the cigars that he sent him in exchange for the little boxes of leaf—eat them, smoke them, smell them, roll in them or rub them in his hair? If he had hair, of course.

He shook his head and closed the door and went out into the hall, being doubly sure that his door was locked behind him. He would not put it past his neighbors, especially the Widow Foshay, to sneak in behind his back.

The hall was empty and he was glad of that. He rang almost stealthily for the elevator, hoping that his luck would hold.

It didn't.

Down the hall came the neighbor from next door. He was the loud and flashy kind, and without any encouragement at all, he'd slap one on the back.

"Good morning, Clyde!" he bellowed happily from afar.

"Good morning, Mr. Morton," Packer replied, somewhat icily. Morton had no right to call him Clyde. No one ever called him Clyde, except sometimes his nephew, Anton Camper, called him Uncle Clyde, although he mostly called him Unk. And Tony, Packer reminded himself, was a worthless piece—always involved in some fancy scheme, always talking big, but without much to show for it. And besides, Tony was crooked—as crooked as a cat.

Like myself, Packer thought, exactly like myself. Not like the most of the rest of them these days, who measured to no more than just loud-talking boobies.

In my day, he told himself with fond remembrance, *I could have skinned them all and they'd never know it until I twitched their hides slick off.*

"How is the stamp business this morning?" yelled Morton, coming up and clapping Packer soundly on the back.

"I must remind you, Mr. Morton, that I am not in the stamp business," Packer told him sharply. "I am interested in stamps and I find it most absorbing and I could highly recommend it—"

"But that is not what I meant," explained Morton, rather taken aback. "I didn't mean you dealt in stamps ..."

"As a matter of fact, I do," said Packer, "to a limited extent. But not as a regular thing and certainly not as a regular business. There are certain other collectors who are aware of my connections and sometimes seek me out—"

"That's the stuff!" boomed Morton, walloping him on the back again in sheer good fellowship. "If you have the right connections, you get along okay. That works in any line. Now, take mine, for instance ..."

The elevator arrived and rescued Packer.

In the lobby, he headed for the desk.

"Good morning, Mr. Packer," said the clerk, handing him some letters. "There is a bag for you and it runs slightly heavy. Do you want me to get someone to help you with it?"

"No, thank you," Packer said. "I am sure that I can manage."

The clerk hoisted the bag atop the counter and Packer seized it and let it fall to the floor. It was fairly large—it weighed, he judged, thirty pounds or so—and the shipping tag, he saw with a thrill of anticipation, was almost covered with stamps of such high denominations they quite took his breath away.

He looked at the tag and saw that his name and address were printed with painful precision, as if the Earthian alphabet was something entirely incomprehensible to the sender. The return address was a mere jumble of dots and hooks and dashes that made no sense, but seemed somewhat familiar, although Packer at the moment was unable to tell exactly what they were. The stamps, he saw, were Iota Cancri, and he had seen stamps such as them only once before in his entire life. He stood there, mentally calculating what their worth might be.

He tucked the letters under his arm and picked up the bag. It was heavier than he had expected and he wished momentarily that he had allowed the clerk to find someone to carry it for him. But he had said that he would carry it and he couldn't very well go back and say he'd rather not. After all, he assured himself, he wasn't quite that old and feeble yet.

He reached the elevator and let the bag down and stood facing the grillwork, waiting for the cage.

A birdlike voice sounded from behind him and he shivered at it, for he recognized the voice—it was the Widow Foshay.

"Why, Mr. Packer," said the Widow, gushingly, "how pleasant to find you waiting here."

He turned around. There was nothing else for it; he couldn't just stand there, with his back to her.

"And so loaded down!" the Widow sympathized. "Here, do let me help you."

She snatched the letters from him.

"There," she said triumphantly, "poor man; I can carry these."

He could willingly have choked her, but he smiled instead. It was a somewhat strained and rather ghastly smile, but he did the best he could.

"How lucky for me," he told her, "that you came along. I'd never have made it."

The veiled rebuke was lost on her. She kept on bubbling at him.

"I'm going to make beef broth for lunch," she said, "and I always make too much. Could I ask you in to share it?"

"Impossible," he told her in alarm. "I am very sorry, but this is my busy day. I have all these, you see." And he motioned at the mail she held and the bag he clutched. He whuffled through his whiskers at her like an irate walrus, but she took no notice.

"How exciting and romantic it must be," she gushed, "getting all these letters and bags and packages from all over the galaxy. From such strange places and from so far away. Some day you must explain to me about stamp collecting."

"Madam," he said a bit stiffly, "I've worked with stamps for more than twenty years and I'm just barely beginning to gain an understanding of what it is all about. I would not presume to explain to someone else."

She kept on bubbling.

Damn it all, he thought, *is there no way to quiet the blasted woman?*

Prying old biddy, he told himself, once again whuffling his whiskers at her. She'd spend the next three days running all about and telling everyone in the entire building about her strange encounter with him and what a strange old coot he was. "Getting all those letters from all those alien places," she would say, "and bags and packages as well. You can't tell me that stamps are the only things in which he's interested. There is more to it than that; you can bet your bottom dollar on it."

At his door she reluctantly gave him back his letters.

"You won't reconsider on that broth?" she asked him. "It's more than just ordinary broth. I pride myself on it. A special recipe."

"I'm sorry," he said.

He unlocked his door and started to open it. She remained standing there.

"I'd like to invite you in," he told her, lying like a gentleman, "but I simply can't. The place is a bit upset."

Upset was somewhat of an understatement.

Safely inside, he threaded his way among piles of albums, boxes, bags and storage cases scattered everywhere.

He finally reached the desk and dropped the bag beside it. He leafed through the letters and one was from Dahib and another was from the Lyraen system and the third from Muphrid, while the remaining one was an advertisement from a concern out on Mars.

He sat down in the massive, upholstered chair behind his desk and surveyed the room.

Someday he'd have to get it straightened out, he told himself. Undoubtedly there was a lot of junk he could simply throw away and the rest of it should be boxed and labeled so that he could lay his hands upon it. It might be, as well, a good idea to make out a general inventory sheet so that he'd have some idea what he had and what it might be worth.

Although, he thought, the value of it was not of so great a moment.

He probably should specialize, he thought. That was what most collectors did. The galaxy was much too big to try to collect it all. Even back a couple of thousand years ago when all the collectors had to worry about were the stamps of Earth, the field even then had become so large and so unwieldy and so scattered that specialization had become the thing.

But what would a man specialize in if he should decide to

restrict his interest? Perhaps just the stamps from one particular planet or one specific system? Perhaps only stamps from beyond a certain distance—say, five hundred light-years? Or covers, perhaps? A collection of covers with postmarks and cancellations showing the varying intricacies of letter communication throughout the depths of space, from star to star, could be quite interesting.

And that was the trouble with it—it all was so interesting. A man could spend three full lifetimes at it and still not reach the end of it.

In twenty years, he told himself, a man could amass a lot of material if he applied himself. And he had applied himself; he had worked hard at it and enjoyed every minute of it, and had become in certain areas, he thought with pride, somewhat of an expert. On occasion he had written articles for the philatelic press, and scarcely a week went by that some man well-known in the field did not drop by for a chat or to seek his aid in a knotty problem.

There was a lot of satisfaction to be found in stamps, he told himself with apologetic smugness. Yes, sir, a great deal of satisfaction.

But the mere collection of material was only one small part of it—a sort of starting point. Greater than all the other facets of it were the contacts that one made. For one had to make contacts—especially out in the farther reaches of the galaxy. Unless one wanted to rely upon the sorry performance of the rascally dealers, who offered only what was easy to obtain, one must establish contacts. Contacts with other collectors who might be willing to trade stamps with one; contacts with lonely men in lonely outposts far out on the rim, where the really exotic material was most likely to turn up, and who would be willing to watch for it and save it and send it on to one at a realistic price; with farout institutions that made up mixtures and job lots in an attempt to eke out a miserly budget voted by the home communities.

There was a man by the name of Marsh out in the Coonskin system who wanted no more than the latest music tapes from Earth for the material that he sent along. And the valiant priest at the missionary station on barren Agustron who wanted old tobacco tins and empty bottles which, for a most peculiar reason, had high value on that topsy-turvy world. And

52

among the many others, Earthmen and aliens alike, there was always PugAlNash.

Packer rolled the wad of leaf across his tongue, sucking out the last faded dregs of its tantalizing flavor.

If a man could make a deal for a good-sized shipment of the leaf, he thought, he could make a fortune on it. Packaged in small units, like packs of gum, it would go like hot cakes here on Earth. He had tried to bring up the subject with Pug, but had done no more than confuse and perplex the good Unukian who, for some unfathomable reason, could not conceive of any commerce that went beyond the confines of simple barter to meet the personal needs of the bargaining individuals.

The doorbell chimed and Packer went to answer it.

It was Tony Camper.

"Hi, Uncle Clyde," said Tony breezily.

Packer held the door open grudgingly.

"Since you are here," he said, "you might as well come in."

Tony stepped in and tilted his hat back on his head. He looked the apartment over with an appraising eye.

"Some day, Unk," he said, "you should get this place shoveled out. I don't see how you stand it."

"I manage it quite well," Packer informed him tartly. "Some day I'll get around to straightening up a bit."

"I should hope you do," said Tony.

"My boy," said Packer, with a trace of pride, "I think that I can say, without fear of contradiction, that I have one of the finest collections of out-star stamps that anyone can boast. Some day, when I get them all in albums—"

"You'll never make it, Unk. It'll just keep piling up. It comes in faster than you can sort it out."

He reached out a foot and nudged the bag beside the desk.

"Like this," he said. "This is a new one, isn't it?"

"It just came in," admitted Packer. "Haven't gotten around as yet to figuring out exactly where it's from."

"Well, that is fine," said Tony. "Keep on having fun. You'll outlive us all."

"Sure I will," said Packer testily. "What is it that you want?"

"Not a thing, Unk. Just dropped in to say hello and to remind you you're coming up to Hudson's to spend the weekend with us. Ann insisted that I drop around and nudge you. The kids have been counting the days—"

"I would have remembered it," lied Packer, who had quite forgotten it.

"I could drop around and pick you up. Three this afternoon?"

"No, Tony, don't bother. I'll catch a stratocab. I couldn't leave that early. I have things to do."

"I bet you have," said Tony.

He moved toward the door.

"You won't forget," he cautioned.

"No, of course I won't," snapped Packer.

"Ann would be plenty sore if you did. She's fixing everything you like."

Packer grunted at him.

"Dinner at seven," said Tony cheerfully.

"Sure, Tony. I'll be there."

"See you, Unk," said Tony, and was gone.

Young whippersnapper, Packer told himself. *Wonder what he's up to now. Always got a new deal cooking, never quite making out on it. Just keeps scraping along.*

He stumped back to the desk.

Figures he'll be getting my money when I die, he thought. *The little that I have. Well, I'll fool him. I'll spend every cent of it. I'll manage to live long enough for that.*

He sat down and picked up one of the letters, slit it open with his pocketknife and dumped out its contents on the one small bare spot on the desk in front of him.

He snapped on the desk lamp and pulled it close. He bent above the stamps.

Pretty fair lot, he thought. That one there from Rho Geminorum XII, or was it XVI, was a fine example of the modern classic—designed with delicacy and imagination, engraved with loving care and exactitude, laid on paper of the highest quality, printed with the highest technical precision.

He hunted for his stamp tongs and failed to find them. He opened the desk drawer and rummaged through the tangled rat's nest he found inside it. He got down on his hands and knees and searched beneath the desk.

He didn't find the tongs.

He got back, puffing, into his chair, and sat there angrily.

Always losing tongs, he thought. *I bet this is the twentieth pair I've lost. Just can't keep track of them, damn 'em!*

The door chimed.

"Well, come on in!" Packer yelled in wrath.

A mouselike little man came in and closed the door gently behind him. He stood timidly just inside, twirling his hat between his hands.

"You Mr. Packer, sir?"

"Yes, sure I am," yelled Packer. "Who did you expect to find here?"

"Well, sir," said the man, advancing a few careful steps into the room, "I am Jason Pickering. You may have heard of me."

"Pickering?" said Packer. "Pickering? Oh, sure, I've heard of you. You're the one who specializes in Polaris."

"That is right," admitted Pickering, mincing just a little. "I am gratified that you—"

"Not at all," said Packer, getting up to shake his hand. "I'm the one who's honored."

He bent and swept two albums and three shoe boxes off a chair. One of the shoe boxes tipped over and a mound of stamps poured out.

"Please have a chair, Mr. Pickering," Packer said majestically.

Pickering, his eyes popping slightly, sat down gingerly on the edge of the swept-clean chair.

"My, my," he said, his eyes taking in the litter that filled the apartment, "you seem to have a lot of stuff here. Undoubtedly, however, you can lay your hands on anything you want."

"Not a chance," said Packer, sitting down again. "I have no idea whatsoever what I have."

Pickering tittered. "Then, sir, you may well be in for some wonderful surprises."

"I'm never surprised at anything," said Packer loftily.

"Well, on to business," said Pickering. "I do not mean to waste your time. I was wondering if it were possible you might have Polaris 17b on cover. It's quite an elusive number, even off cover, and I know of not a single instance of one that's tied to cover. But someone was telling me that perhaps you might have one tucked away."

"Let me see, now," said Packer. He leaned back in his chair

55

and leafed catalogue pages rapidly through his mind. And suddenly he had it—Polaris 17b—a tiny stamp, almost a midget stamp, bright blue with a tiny crimson dot in the lower left-hand corner and its design a mass of lacy scrollwork.

"Yes," he said, opening his eyes, "I believe I may have one. I seem to remember, years ago . . ."

Pickering leaned forward, hardly breathing.

"You mean you actually . . ."

"I'm sure it's here somewhere," said Packer, waving his hand vaguely at the room.

"If you find it," offered Pickering, "I'll pay ten thousand for it."

"A strip of five," said Packer, "as I remember it. Out of Polaris VII to Betelgeuse XIII by way of—I don't seem to remember by way of where."

"A strip of five!"

"As I remember it. I might be mistaken."

"Fifty thousand," said Pickering, practically frothing at the mouth. "Fifty thousand, if you find it."

Packer yawned. "For only fifty thousand, Mr. Pickering, I wouldn't even look."

"A hundred, then."

"I might think about it."

"You'll start looking right away? You must have some idea."

"Mr. Pickering, it has taken me all of twenty years to pile up all the litter that you see and my memory's not too good. I'd have not the slightest notion where to start."

"Set your price," urged Pickering. "What do you want for it?"

"If I find it," said Packer, "I might consider a quarter million. That is, if I find it."

"You'll look?"

"I'm not sure. Some day I might stumble on it. Some day I'll have to clean up the place. I'll keep an eye out for it."

Pickering stood up stiffly.

"You jest with me," he said.

Packer waved a feeble hand, "I never jest," he said.

Pickering moved toward the door.

Packer heaved himself from the chair.

"I'll let you out," he said.

"Never mind. And thank you very much."

Packer eased himself back into the chair and watched the man go out.

He sat there, trying to remember where the Polaris cover might be buried. And finally gave up. It had been so long ago.

He hunted some more for the tongs, but he didn't find them.

He'd have to go out first thing in the morning and buy another pair. Then he remembered that he wouldn't be here in the morning. He'd be up on Hudson's Bay, at Tony's summer place.

It did beat hell, he thought, how he could manage to lose so many tongs.

He sat for a long time, letting himself sink into a sort of suspended state, not quite asleep, nor yet entirely awake, and he thought, quite vaguely and disjointedly, of many curious things.

But mostly about adhesive postage stamps and how, of all the ideas exported by the Earth, the idea of the use of stamps had caught on most quickly and, in the last two thousand years, had spread to the far corners of the galaxy.

It was getting hard, he told himself, to keep track of all the stamps, even of the planets that were issuing stamps. There were new ones popping up all the blessed time. A man must keep everlastingly on his toes to keep tab on all of them.

There were some funny stamps, he thought. Like the ones from Menkalinen that used smells to spell out their values. Not five cent stamps or five dollar stamps or hundred dollar stamps, but one stamp that smelled something like a pasture rose for the local mail and another stamp that had the odor of ripe old cheese for the system mail and yet another with a stink that could knock out a human at forty paces distance for the interstellar service.

And the Algeiban issues that shifted into colors beyond the range of human vision—and worst of all, with the values based on that very shift of color. And that famous classic issue put out, quite illegally, of course, by the Leonidian pirates who had used, instead of paper, the well-tanned, thin-scraped hides of human victims who had fallen into their clutches.

He sat nodding in the chair, listening to a clock hidden somewhere behind the litter of the room, ticking loudly in the silence.

It made a good life, he told himself, a very satisfactory life. Twenty years ago when Myra had died and he had sold his interest in the export company, he'd been ready to curl up and end it all, ready to write off his life as one already lived. But today, he thought, he was more absorbed in stamps than he'd ever been in the export business and it was a blessing—that was what it was, a blessing.

He sat there and thought kindly of his stamps, which had rescued him from the deep wells of loneliness, which had given back his life and almost made him young again.

And then he fell asleep.

The door chimes wakened him and he stumbled to the door, rubbing sleep out of his eyes.

The Widow Foshay stood in the hall, with a small kettle in her hands. She held it out to him.

"I thought, poor man, he will enjoy this," she said. "It's some of the beef broth that I made. And I always make so much. It's so hard to cook for one."

Packer took the kettle.

"It was kind of you," he mumbled.

She looked at him sharply.

"You are sick," she said.

She stepped through the door, forcing him to step back, forcing her way in.

"Not sick," he protested limply. "I fell asleep, that's all. There's nothing wrong with me."

She reached out a pudgy hand and held it on his forehead.

"You have a fever," she declared. "You are burning up."

"There's nothing wrong with me," he bellowed. "I tell you, I just fell asleep, is all."

She turned and bustled out into the room, threading her way among the piled-up litter. Watching her, he thought: *My God, she finally got into the place! How can I throw her out?*

"You come over here and sit right down," she ordered him. "I don't suppose you have a thermometer."

He shook his head, defeated.

"Never had any need of one," he said. "Been healthy all my life."

She screamed and jumped and whirled around and headed for the door at an awkward gallop. She stumbled across a pile of boxes and fell flat upon her face, then scrambled, screeching, to her feet and shot out of the door.

Packer slammed the door behind her and stood looking, with some fascination, at the kettle in his hand. Despite all the ruckus, he'd spilled not a single drop.

But what had caused the Widow ...

Then he saw it—a tiny mouse running on the floor.

He hoisted the kettle in a grave salute.

"Thanks, my friend," he said.

He made his way to the table in the dining room and found a place where he could put down the kettle.

Mice, he thought. There had been times when he had suspected that he had them—nibbled cheese on the kitchen shelf, scurryings in the night—and he had worried some about them making nests in the material he had stacked all about the place.

But mice had a good side to them, too, he thought.

He looked at his watch and it was almost five o'clock and he had an hour or so before he had to catch a cab and he realized now that somehow he had managed to miss lunch. So he'd have some of the broth and while he was doing that he'd look over the material that was in the bag.

He lifted some of the piled-up boxes off the table and set them on the floor so he had some room to empty the contents of the bag.

He went to the kitchen and got a spoon and sampled the broth. It was more than passing good. It was still warm and he had no doubt that the kettle might do the finish of the table top no good, but that was something one need not worry over.

He hauled the bag over to the table and puzzled out the strangeness of the return address. It was the new script they'd started using a few years back out in the Bootes system and it was from a rather shady gentle-being from one of the Cygnian stars who appreciated, every now and then, a case of the finest Scotch.

Packer, hefting the bag, made a mental note to ship him two, at least.

He opened up the bag and upended it and a mound of covers flowed out on the table.

Packer tossed the bag into a corner and sat down contentedly. He sipped at the broth and began going slowly through the pile of covers. They were, by and large, magnificent. Someone had taken the trouble to try to segregate them according to systems of their origin and had arranged them in little packets, held in place by rubber bands.

There was a packet from Rasalhague and another from Cheleb and from Nunki and Kaus Borealis and from many other places.

And there was a packet of others he did not recognize at all. It was a fairly good-sized packet with twenty-five or thirty covers in it and all the envelopes, he saw, were franked with the same stamps—little yellow fellows that had no discernible markings on them—just squares of yellow paper, rather thick and rough. He ran his thumb across one and he got the sense of crumbling, as if the paper were soft and chalky and were abrading beneath the pressure of his thumb.

Fascinated, he pulled one envelope from beneath the rubber band and tossed the rest of the packet to one side.

He shambled to his desk and dug frantically in the drawer and came back with a glass. He held it above the stamp and peered through it and he had been right—there were no markings on the stamp. It was a mere yellow square of paper that was rather thick and pebbly, as if it were made up of tiny grains of sand.

He straightened up and spooned broth into his mouth and frantically flipped the pages of his mental catalogue, but he got no clue. So far as he could recall, he'd never seen or heard of that particular stamp before.

He examined the postmarks with the glass and some of them he could recognize and there were others that he couldn't, but that made no difference, for he could look them up, at a later time, in one of the postmark and cancellation handbooks. He got the distinct impression, however, that the planet, or planets, of origin must lie Libra-ward, for all the postmarks he could recognize trended in that direction.

He laid the glass away and turned his full attention to the broth, being careful of his whiskers. Whiskers, he reminded himself, were no excuse for one to be a sloppy eater.

The spoon turned in his hand at that very moment and some of the broth spilled down his beard and some spattered on the table, but the most of it landed on the cover with the yellow stamp.

He pulled a handkerchief from his pocket and tried to wipe the cover clean, but it wouldn't wipe. The envelope was soggy and the stamp was ruined with the grease and he said a few choice cusswords, directed at his clumsiness.

Then he took the dripping cover by one corner and hunted until he found the wastebasket and dropped the cover in it.

He was glad to get back from the weekend at Hudson's Bay.

Tony was a fool, he thought, to sink so much money in such a fancy place. He had no more prospects than a rabbit and his high pressure deals always seemed to peter out, but he still went on talking big and hung onto that expensive summer place. Maybe, Packer thought, that was the way to do it these days; maybe if you could fool someone into thinking you were big, you might have a better chance of getting into something big. Maybe that was the way it worked, but he didn't know.

He stopped in the lobby to pick up his mail, hoping there might be a package from PugAlNash. In the excitement of leaving for the weekend, he'd forgotten to take along the box of leaf and three days without it had impressed upon him how much he had come to rely upon it. Remembering how low his supply was getting, he became a little jittery to think that more might not be forthcoming.

There was a batch of letters, but no box from Pug.

And he might have known, he told himself, that there wouldn't be, for the box never came until he was entirely out. At first, he recalled, he wondered by what prophetic insight Pug might have known when the leaf was gone, how he could have gauged the shipping time to have it arrive exactly when there was need of it. But now he no longer thought about it, for it was one of those unbelievable things it does no good to think about.

"Glad to have you back," the clerk told him cheerfully. "You had a good weekend, Mr. Packer?"

"Tolerable," growled Packer, grumpily, heading for the elevator.

Before he reached it, he was apprehended by Elmer Lang, the manager of the building.

"Mr. Packer," he whinnied, "I'd like to talk to you."

"Well, go ahead and talk."

"It's about the mice, Mr. Packer."

"What mice?"

"Mrs. Foshay tells me there are mice in your apartment."

Packer drew himself up to the fullness of his rather dumpy height.

"They are your mice, Lang," he said. "You get rid of them."

Lang wrung his hands. "But how can I, Mr. Packer? It's the way you keep your place. All that litter in there. You've got to clean it up."

"That litter, I'll have you know, sir, is probably one of the most unique stamp collections in the entire galaxy. I've gotten behind a little in keeping it together, true, but I will not have you call it litter."

"I could have Miles, the caretaker, help you get it straightened out."

"I tell you, sir," said Packer, "the only one who could help me is one trained in philately. Does your caretaker happen to be—"

"But, Mr. Packer," Lang pleaded, "all that paper and all those boxes are nesting places for them. I can do nothing about the mice unless I can get in there and get some of it cleared away."

"Cleared away!" exploded Packer. "Do you realize, sir, what you are talking of? Somewhere hidden in that vast stock of material, is a certain cover—to you, sir, an envelope with stamps and postmarks on it—for which I have been offered a quarter million dollars if I ever turn it up. And that is one small piece of all the material I have there. I ask you, Lang, is that the sort of stuff that you clear away?"

"But, Mr. Packer, I cannot allow it to go on. I must insist—"

The elevator arrived and Packer stalked into it haughtily, leaving the manager standing in the lobby, twisting at his hands.

Packer whuffled his moustache at the operator.

"Busybody," he said.

"What was that, sir?"

"Mrs. Foshay, my man. She's a busybody."

"I do believe," said the operator judiciously, "that you may be entirely right."

Packer hoped the corridor would be empty and it was. He unlocked his door and stepped inside.

A bubbling noise stopped him in his tracks.

He stood listening, unbelieving, just a little frightened.

The bubbling noise went on and on.

He stepped cautiously out into the room and as he did he saw it.

The wastebasket beside the desk was full of a bubbling yellow stuff that in several places had run down the sides and formed puddles on the floor.

Packer stalked the basket, half prepared to turn and run.

But nothing happened. The yellowness in the basket simply kept on bubbling.

It was a rather thick and gooey mess, not frothy, and the bubbling was no more than a noise that it was making, for in the strict sense of the word, he saw, it was not bubbling.

Packer sidled closer and thrust out a hand toward the basket. It did not snap at him. It paid no attention to him.

He poked a finger at it and the stuff was fairly solid and slightly warm and he got the distinct impression that it was alive.

And immediately he thought of the broth-soaked cover he had thrown in the basket. It was not so unusual that he should think of it, for the yellow of the brew within the basket was the exact color of the stamp upon the cover.

He walked around the desk and dropped the mail he'd picked up in the lobby. He sat down ponderously in the massive office chair.

So a stamp had come to life, he thought, and that certainly was a queer one. But no more queer, perhaps, than the properties of many other stamps, for while Earth had exported the idea of their use, a number of peculiar adaptations of the idea had evolved.

And now, he thought a little limply, *I'll have to get this mess in the basket out of here before Lang comes busting in.*

He worried a bit about what Lang had said about cleaning up the place and he got slightly sore about it, for he paid good money for these diggings and he paid promptly in advance and he was never any bother. And besides, he'd been here for twenty years, and Lang should consider that.

He finally got up from the chair and lumbered around the desk. He bent and grasped the wastebasket, being careful to miss the places where the yellow goo had run down the sides. He tried to lift it and the basket did not move. He tugged as hard as he could pull and the basket stayed exactly where it was. He squared off and aimed a kick at it and the basket didn't budge.

He stood off a ways and glared at it, with his whiskers bristling. As if he didn't have all the trouble that he needed, without this basket deal! Somehow or other, he was going to have to get the apartment straightened out and get rid of the mice. He should be looking for the Polaris cover. And he'd lost or mislaid his tongs and would have to waste his time going out to get another pair.

But first of all, he'd have to get this basket out of here. Somehow it had become stuck to the floor—maybe some of the yellow goo had run underneath the edge of it and dried. Maybe if he had a pinch bar or some sort of lever that he could jab beneath it, he could pry it loose.

From the basket the yellow stuff made merry bubbling noises at him.

He clapped his hat back on his head and went out and slammed and locked the door behind him.

It was a fine summer day and he walked around a little, trying to run his many problems throught his mind, but no matter what he thought of, he always came back to the basket brimming with the yellow mess and he knew he'd never be able to get started on any of the other tasks until he got rid of it.

So he hunted up a hardware store and bought a good-sized pinch bar and headed back for the apartment house. The bar, he knew, might mark up the floor somewhat, but if he could get under the edge of the basket with a bar that size he was sure that he could pry it loose.

In the lobby, Lang descended on him.

"Mr. Packer," he said sternly, "where are you going with that bar?"

"I went out and bought it to exterminate the mice."

"But, Mr. Packer—"

"You want to get rid of those mice, don't you?"

"Why, certainly I do."

"It's a desperate situation," Packer told him gravely, "and one that may require very desperate measures."

"But that bar!"

"I'll exercise my best discretion," Packer promised him. "I shall hit them easy."

He went up the elevator with the bar. The sight of Lang's discomfiture made him feel a little better and he managed to whistle a snatch of tune as he went down the hall.

As he fumbled with the key, he heard the sound of rustling coming from beyond the door and he felt a chill go through him, for the rustlings were of a furtive sort and they sounded ominous.

Good Lord, he thought, *there can't be that many mice in there!*

He grasped the bar more firmly and unlocked the door and pushed it open.

The inside of the place was a storm of paper.

He stepped in quickly and slammed the door behind him to keep the blowing paper from swooping out into the hall.

Must have left a window open, he thought. But he knew he had not, and even if he had, it was quiet outside. There was not a breath of breeze.

And what was happening inside the apartment was more than just a breeze.

He stood with his back against the door and watched what was going on and shifted his grip on the bar so that it made a better club.

The apartment was filled with a sleet of flying paper and a barrage of packets and a snowstorm of dancing stamps. There were open boxes standing on the floor and the paper and the stamps and packets were drifting down and chunking into these, and along the wall were other boxes, very neatly piled—and that was entirely wrong, for there had been nothing neat about the place when he had left it less than two hours before.

But even as he watched, the activity slacked off. There was less stuff flying through the air and some of the boxes were closed by unseen hands and then flew off, all by themselves, to stack themselves with the other boxes.

Poltergeists! he thought in terror, his mind scrambling back frantically over all that he had ever thought or read or heard to grasp some explanation.

Then it was done and over.

There was nothing flying through the air. All the boxes had been stacked. Everything was still.

Packer stepped out into the room and stared in slack-jawed amazement.

The desk and the tables shone. The drapes hung straight and clean. The carpeting looked as if it might be new. Chairs and small tables and lamps and other things, long forgotten, buried all these years beneath the accumulation of his collection, stood revealed and shining—dusted, cleaned and polished.

And in the middle of all this righteous order stood the wastebasket, bubbling happily.

Packer dropped the bar and headed for the desk.

In front of him a window flapped open and he heard a swish and the bar went past him, flying for the window. It went out the window and slashed through the foliage of a tree, then the window closed and he lost sight of it.

Packer took off his hat and tossed it on the desk.

Immediately his hat lifted from the desk and sailed for a closet door. The closet door swung open and the hat ducked in. The door closed gently on it.

Packer whuffled through his whiskers. He got out his handkerchief and mopped a glistening brow.

"Funny goings-on," he said to himself.

Slowly, cautiously, he checked the place. All the boxes were stacked along one wall, three deep and piled from floor to ceiling. Three filing cabinets stood along another wall and he rubbed his eyes at that, for he had forgotten that there were three of them—for years he'd thought that he had only two. And all the rest of the place was neat and clean and it fairly gleamed.

He walked from room to room and everywhere it was the same.

In the kitchen the pots and pans were all in place and the dishes stacked primly in the cupboard. The stove and refigerator had been wiped clean and there were no dirty dishes and that was a bit surprising for he was sure there had been. Mrs. Foshay's kettle, with the broth emptied out of it and scrubbed until it shone, stood on the kitchen table.

He went back to the desk and the top of it was clear except for several items laid out, as if for his attention:

Ten dead mice.

Eight pairs of stamp tongs.

The packet of covers with the strange yellow stamps.

Two—not one—but two covers, one bearing a strip of four and the other a strip of five Polaris 17b.

Packer sat down heavily in his chair and stared at the items on the desk.

How in the world, he wondered—how had it come about? What was going on?

He peeked around the desk edge at the bubbling basket and it seemed to chortle at him.

It was, he told himself, it *must be* the basket—or, rather, the stuff within the basket. Nothing else had been changed, no other factor had been added. The only thing new and different in the apartment was the basket of yellow gook.

He picked up the packet of covers with the yellow stamps affixed and opened the drawer to find a glass. The drawer was arranged with startling neatness and there were five glasses lying in a row. He chose the strongest one.

Beneath the glass the surface of the stamps became a field made up of tiny ball-like particles, unlike the grains of sand which the weaker glass he had used before had shown.

He bent above the desk, with his eye glued to the glass, and he knew that what he was looking at were spores.

Encysted, lifeless, they still would carry life within them, and that had been what had happened here. He'd spilled the broth upon the stamp and the spores had come to life—a strange alien community of life that settled within the basket.

He put the glass back in the drawer and rose. He gathered up the dead mice carefully by their tails. He carried them to the incinerator shaft and let them drop.

He crossed the room to the bookcases and the books were arranged in order and in sequence and there, finally, were books that he'd lost years ago and hunted ever since. There were long rows of stamp catalogs, the set of handbooks on galactic cancellations, the massive list of postmarks, the galactic travel guides, the long row of weird language dictionaries, indispensable in alien stamp identification, and a number of technical works on philatelic subjects.

From the bookcase he moved to the piled-up boxes. One of them he lifted down. It was filled with covers, with glassine envelopes of loose stamps, with sheets, with blocks and strips. He dug through the contents avidly, with wonder mounting in him.

All the stamps, all the covers, were from the Thuban system. He closed the box and bent to lift it back. It didn't wait for him. It lifted by itself and fitted itself in place.

He looked at three more boxes. One contained, exclusively, material from Korephoros, and another material from Antares and the third from Dschubba. Not only had the litter been picked up and boxed and piled into some order, but the material itself had been roughly classified!

He went back to the chair and sat down a little weakly. It was too much, he thought, for a man to take.

The spores had fed upon the broth and had come to life, and within the basket was an alien life form or a community of life forms. And they possessed a passion for orderliness and a zest for work and an ability to channel that zest into useful channels.

And what was more, the things within the basket did what a man wanted done.

It had straightened up the apartment, it had classified the stamps and covers, it had killed the mice, it had located the Polaris covers and had found the missing tongs.

And how had it known that he wanted these things done? Read his mind, perhaps?

He shivered at the thought, but the fact remained that it had done absolutely nothing except bubble merrily away until he had returned. It had done nothing, perhaps, because it did not know what to do—until he had somehow told it what to do. For as soon as he had returned, it had found out what to do and did it.

The door chimed and he got up to answer.

It was Tony.

"Hi, Unk," he said. "You forgot your pajamas and I brought them back. You left them on the bed and forgot to pack them."

He held out a package and it wasn't until then that he saw the room.

"Unk!" he yelled. "What happened? You got the place cleaned up!"

Packer shook his head in bewilderment. "Something funny, Tony."

Tony walked in and stared around in admiration and astonishment.

"You sure did a job," he said.

"I didn't do it, Tony."

"Oh, I see. You hired someone to do it while you were up at our place."

"No, not that. It was done this morning. It was done by that!"

He pointed at the basket.

"You're crazy, Unk," said Tony, firmly. "You have flipped your thatch."

"Maybe so," said Packer. "But the basket did the work."

Tony walked around the basket warily. He reached down and punched the yellow stuff with a stuck-out finger.

"It feels like dough," he announced.

He straightened up and looked at Packer.

"You aren't kidding me?" he asked.

"I don't know what it is," said Packer. "I don't know why or how it did it, but I'm telling you the truth."

"Unk," said Tony, "we may have something here!"

"There is no doubt of that."

"No, that's not what I mean. This may be the biggest thing that ever happened. This junk, you say, will really work for you?"

"Somehow or other," said Packer. "I don't know how it does it. It has a sense of order and it does the work you want. It seems to understand you—it anticipates whatever you want done. Maybe it's a brain with enormous psi powers. I was looking at a cover the other night and I saw this yellow stamp ..."

Packer told him swiftly what had happened.

Tony listened thoughtfully, pulling at his chin.

"Well, all right, Unk," he said, "we've got it. We don't know what it is or how it works, but let's put our thinking into gear. Just imagine a bucket of this stuff standing in an office—a great big, busy office. It would make for efficiency such as you never saw before. It would file all the papers and keep the records straight and keep the entire business strictly up to date. There'd never be anything ever lost again. Everything would be right where it was supposed to be and could be located in a second. When the boss or someone else should want a certain file—bingo! it would be upon his desk. Why, an office with one of these little buckets could get rid of all its file clerks. A public library could be run efficiently without any personnel at all. But

69

it would be in big business offices—in insurance firms and industrial concerns and transportation companies—where it would be worth the most."

Packer shook his head, a bit confused. "It might be all right, Tony; it might work the way you say. But who would believe you? Who would pay attention? It's just too fantastic. They would laugh at you."

"You leave all that to me," said Tony. "That's my end of the business. That's where I come in."

"Oh," said Packer, "so we're in business now."

"I have a friend," said Tony, who always had a friend, "who'd let me try it out. We could put a bucket of this stuff in his office and see how it works out."

He looked around, suddenly all business.

"You got a bucket, Unk?"

"Out in the kitchen. You'd find something there."

"And beef broth. It was beef broth, wasn't it?"

Packer nodded. "I think I have a can of it."

Tony stood and scratched his head. "Now let's get this figured out, Unk. What we want is a sure source of supply."

"I have those other covers. They all have stamps on them. We could start a new batch with one of them."

Tony gestured impatiently. "No, that wouldn't do. They are our reserves. We lock them tight away against emergency. I have a hunch that we can grow bucket after bucket of the stuff from what we have right here. Pull off a handful of it and feed it a shot of broth—"

"But how do you know—"

"Unk," said Tony, "doesn't it strike you a little funny that you had the exact number of spores in that one stamp, the correct amount of broth, to grow just one basket full?"

"Well, sure, but ..."

"Look, this stuff is intelligent. It knows what it is doing. It lays down rules for itself to live by. It's got a sense of order and it lives by order. So you give it a wastebasket to live in and it lives within the limits of that basket. It gets just level with the top; it lets a little run down the sides to cement the basket tight to the floor. And that is all. It doesn't run over. It doesn't fill the room. It has some discipline."

"Well, maybe you are right, but that still doesn't answer the question—"

"Just a second, Unk. Watch here."

Tony plunged his hand into the basket and came out with a chunk of the spore-growth ripped loose from the parent body.

"Now, watch the basket, Unk," he said.

They watched. Swiftly, the spores surged and heaved to fill the space where the ripped-out chunk had been. Once again the basket was very neatly filled.

"You see what I mean?" said Tony. "Given more living room, it will grow. All we have to do is feed it so it can. And we'll give it living room. We'll give it a lot of buckets, so it can grow to its heart's content and—"

"Damn it, Tony, will you listen to me? I been trying to ask you what we're going to do to keep it from cementing itself to the floor. If we start another batch of it, it will cement its bucket or its basket or whatever it is in to the floor just like this first one did."

"I'm glad you brought that up," said Tony. "I know just what to do. We will hang it up. We'll hang up the bucket and there won't be any floor."

"Well," said Packer, "I guess that covers it. I'll go heat up that broth."

They heated the broth and found a bucket and hung it on a broomstick suspended between two chairs.

They dropped the chunk of spore-growth in and watched it and it stayed just as it was.

"My hunch was right," said Tony. "It needs some of that broth to get it started."

He poured in some broth and the spores melted before their very eyes into a black and ropy scum.

"There's something wrong," said Tony, worriedly.

"I guess there is," said Packer.

"I got an idea, Unk. You might have used a different brand of broth. There might be some difference in the ingredients. It may not be the broth itself, but some ingredient in it that gives this stuff the shot in the arm it needs. We might be using the wrong broth."

Packer shuffled uncomfortably.

"I don't remember, Tony."

"You have to!" Tony yelled at him. "Think, Unk! You got to—you have to remember what brand it was you used." Packer whuffled out his whiskers unhappily.

"Well, to tell you the truth, Tony, it wasn't bought broth. Mrs. Foshay made it."

"Now we're getting somewhere! Who is Mrs. Foshay?"

"She's a nosy old dame who lives across the hall."

"Well, that's just fine. All you have to do is ask her to make some more for you."

"I can't do it, Tony."

"All we'd need is one batch, Unk. We could have it analyzed and find out what is in it. Then we'd be all set."

"She'd want to know why I wanted it. And she'd tell all over how I asked for it. She might even figure out there was something funny going on."

"We can't have that," exclaimed Tony in alarm. "This is our secret, Unk. We can't cut in anyone."

He sat and thought.

"Anyhow, she's probably sore at me," said Packer. "She sneaked in the other day and got the hell scared out of her when a mouse ran across the floor. She tore down to the management about it and tried to make me trouble."

Tony snapped his fingers.

"I got it!" he cried. "I know just how we'll work it. You go on and get in bed—"

"I will not!" snarled Packer.

"Now listen, Unk, you have to play along. You have to do you part."

"I don't like it," protested Packer. "I don't like any part of it."

"You get in bed," insisted Tony, "and look the worst you can. Pretend you're suffering. I'll go over to this Mrs. Foshay and I'll tell her how upset you were over that mouse scaring her. I'll say you worked all day to get the place cleaned up just because of that. I'll say you worked so hard—"

"You'll do no such thing," yelped Packer. "She'll come tearing in here. I won't have that woman—"

"You want to make a couple billion, don't you?" asked Tony angrily.

"I don't care particularly," Packer told him. "I can't somehow get my heart in it."

"I'll tell this woman that you are all tuckered out and that your heart is not so good and the only thing you want is another bowl of broth."

"You'll tell her no such thing," raved Packer. "You'll leave her out of this."

"Now, Unk," Tony reasoned with him, "if you won't do it for yourself, do it for me—me, the only kin you have in the entire world. It's the first big thing I've ever had a chance at. I may talk a lot and try to look prosperous and successful, but I tell you, Unk ..."

He saw he was getting nowhere.

"Well, if you won't do it for me, do it for Ann, do it for the kids. You wouldn't want to see those poor little kids—"

"Oh, shut up," said Packer. "First thing you know, you'll be blubbering. All right, then, I'll do it."

It was worse than he had thought it would be. If he had known it was to be so bad, he'd never have consented to go through with it.

The Widow Foshay brought the bowl of broth herself. She sat on the bed and held his head up and cooed and crooned at him as she fed him broth.

It was most embarrassing.

But they got what they were after.

When she had finished feeding him, there was still half a bowl of broth and she left that with them because, she said, poor man, he might be needing it.

It was three o'clock in the afternoon and almost time for the Widow Foshay to come in with the broth.

Thinking of it, Packer gagged a little.

Someday, he promised himself, he'd beat Tony's brains out. If it hadn't been for him, this never would have started.

Almost six months now and every blessed day she had brought the broth and sat and talked with him while he forced down a bowl of it. And the worst of it, Packer told himself, was that he had to pretend that he thought that it was good.

And she was so gay! Why did she have to be so gay? *Toujours gai,* he thought. Just like the crazy alley cat that ancient writer had penned the silly lines about.

Garlic in the broth, he thought—*my God, who'd ever heard of garlic in beef broth!* It was uncivilized. A special recipe, she'd said, and it was all of that. And yet it had been the garlic that had done the job with the yellow sporelife—it was the

73

food needed by the spores to kick them into life and to start them growing.

The garlic in the broth might have been good for him as well, he admitted to himself, for in many years, it seemed, he had not felt so fine. There was a spring in his step, he'd noticed, and he didn't get so tired; he used to take a nap in the afternoon and now he never did. He worked as much as ever, actually more than ever, and he was, except for the widow and the broth, a very happy man. Yes, a very happy man.

He would continue to be happy, he told himself, as long as Tony left him to his stamps. Let the little whippersnapper carry the load of Efficiency, Inc.; he was, after all, the one who had insisted on it. Although, to give him credit, he had done well with it. A lot of industries had signed up and a whole raft of insurance companies and a bunch of bond houses and a good scattering of other lines of business. Before long, Tony said, there wouldn't be a business anywhere that would dare to try to get along without the services of Efficiency, Inc.

The doorbell chimed and he went to answer it. It would be the Widow Foshay, and she would have her hands full with the broth.

But it was not the widow.

"Are you Mr. Clyde Packer?" asked the man who stood in the hall.

"Yes, sir," Packer said. "Will you please step in?"

"My name is John Griffin," said the man, after he was seated. "I represent Geneva."

"Geneva? You mean the Government?"

The man showed him credentials.

"Okay," said Packer a bit frostily, being no great admirer of the Government. "What can I do for you?"

"You are senior partner in Efficiency, Inc., I believe."

"I guess that's what I am."

"Mr. Packer, don't you know?"

"Well, I'm not positive. I'm a partner, but I don't know about this senior business. Tony runs the show and I let him have his head."

"You and your nephew are sole owners of the firm?"

"You bet your boots we are. We kept it for ourselves. We took no one in with us."

"Mr. Packer, for some time the Government has been

74

attempting to negotiate with Mr. Camper. He's told you nothing of it?"

"Not a thing," said Packer. "I'm busy with my stamps. He doesn't bother me."

"We have been interested in your service," Griffin said. "We have tried to buy it."

"It's for sale," said Packer. "You just pay the price and—"

"But you don't understand. Mr. Camper insists on a separate contract for every single office that we operate. That would run to a terrific figure—"

"Worth it," Packer assured him. "Every cent of it."

"It's unfair," said Griffin firmly. "We are willing to buy it on a departmental basis and we feel that even in that case we would be making some concession. By rights the Government should be allowed to come in under a single covering arrangement."

"Look," protested Packer, "what are you talking to me for? I don't run the business; Tony does. You'll have to deal with him. I have faith in the boy. He has a good hard business head. I'm not even interested in Efficiency. All I'm interested in is stamps."

"That's just the point," said Griffin heartily. "You've hit the situation exactly on the head."

"Come again?" asked Packer.

"Well, it's like this," Griffin told him in confidential tones. "The Government gets a lot of stamps in its daily correspondence. I forget the figure, but it runs to several tons of philatelic material every day. And from every planet in the galaxy. We have in the past been disposing of it to several stamp concerns, but there's a disposition in certain quarters to offer the whole lot as a package deal at a most attractive price."

"That is fine," said Packer, "but what would I do with several tons a day?"

"I wouldn't know," declared Griffin, "but since you are so interested in stamps, it would give you a splendid opportunity to have first crack at a batch of top-notch material. It is, I dare say, one of the best sources you could find."

"And you'd sell all this stuff to me if I put in a word for you with Tony?"

Griffin grinned happily. "You follow me exactly, Mr. Packer."

Packer snorted, "Follow you! I'm way ahead of you."

"Now, now," cautioned Griffin, "you must not get the wrong impression. This is a business offer—a purely business offer."

"I suppose you'd expect no more than nominal payment for all this waste paper I would be taking off your hands."

"Very nominal," said Griffin.

"All right, I'll think about it and I'll let you know. I can't promise you a thing, of course."

"I understand, Mr. Packer. I do not mean to rush you."

After Griffin left, Packer sat and thought about it and the more he thought about it, the more attractive it became.

He could rent a warehouse and install an Efficiency Basket in it and all he'd have to do would be dump all that junk in there and the basket would sort it out for him.

He wasn't exactly sure if one basket would have the time to break the selection down to more than just planetary groupings, but if one basket couldn't do it, he could install a second one and between the two of them, he could run the classification down to any point he wished. And then, after the baskets had sorted out the more select items for his personal inspection, he could set up an organization to sell the rest of it in job lots and he could afford to sell it at a figure that would run all the rest of those crummy dealers clear out on the limb.

He rubbed his hands together in a gesture of considerable satisfaction, thinking how he could make it rough for all those skinflint dealers. It was murder, he reminded himself, what they got away with; anything that happened to them, they had coming to them.

But there was one thing he gagged on slightly. What Griffin had offered him was little better than a bribe, although it was, he supposed, no more than one could expect of the Government. The entire Governmental structure was loaded with grafters and ten percenters and lobbyists and special interest boys and others of their ilk. Probably no one would think a thing of it if he made the stamp deal—except the dealers, of course, and there was absolutely nothing they could do about it except sit and howl.

But aside from that, he wondered, did he have the right to interfere with Tony? He could mention it to him, of course, and Tony would say yes. But did he have the right?

He sat and worried at the question, without reaching a conclusion, without getting any nearer to the answer, until the door chimes sounded.

It was the Widow Foshay and she was empty-handed. She had no broth today.

"Good afternoon," he said. "You are a little late."

"I was just opening my door to come over when I saw you had a caller. He's gone now, isn't he?"

"For some time," said Packer.

She stepped inside and he closed the door. They walked across the room.

"Mr. Packer," said the Widow, "I must apologize. I brought no broth today. The truth of the matter is, I'm tired of making it all the time."

"In such a case," he said, very gallantly, "the treats will be on me."

He opened the desk drawer and lifted out the brand-new box of PugAlNash's leaf, which had arrived only the day before.

Almost reverently, he lifted the cover and held the box out to her. She recoiled from it a little.

"Go ahead," he urged. "Take a pinch of it. Don't swallow it. Just chew it."

Cautiously, she dipped her fingers in the box.

"That's too much," he warned her. "Just a little pinch. You don't need a lot. And it's rather hard to come by."

She took a pinch and put it in her mouth.

He watched her closely, smiling. She looked for all the world as if she had taken poison. But soon she settled back in her chair, apparently convinced it was not some lethal trick.

"I don't believe," she said, "I've ever tasted anything quite like it."

"You never have. Other than myself, you may well be the only human that has ever tasted it. I get it from a friend of mine who lives on one of the far-out stars. His name is PugAlNash and he sends it regularly. And he always includes a note."

He looked in the drawer and found the latest note.

"Listen to this," he said.

He read it:

Der Fiend: Grately injoid latter smoke you cent me.

*Ples mor of sam agin. You du knot no that I profetick
and wach ahed for you. Butt it be so and I grately hapy
to perform this taske for fiend. I assur you it be onely
four the beste. You prophet grately, maybee.*

Your luving fiend,
PugAlNash

He finished reading it and tossed it on the desk.

"What do you make of it?" he asked. "Especially that crack
about his being a prophet and watching ahead for me?"

"It must be all right," the widow said. "He claims you will
profit greatly."

"He sounds like a gypsy fortune-teller. He had me worried
for a while."

"But why should you worry over that?"

"Because I don't want to know what's going to happen to
me. And sometime he might tell me. If a man could look
ahead, for example, he'd know just when he was going to die
and how and all the—"

"Mr Packer," she told him, "I don't think you're meant to
die. I swear you are getting to look younger every day."

"As a matter of fact," said Packer, vastly pleased, "I'm feeling the best I have in years."

"It may be that leaf he sends you."

"No, I think most likely it is that broth of yours."

They spent a pleasant afternoon—more pleasant, Packer
admitted, than he would have thought was possible.

And after she had left, he asked himself another question
that had him somewhat frightened.

Why in the world, of all people in the world, had he shared
the leaf with her?

He put the box back in the drawer and picked up the note.
He smoothed it out and read it once again.

The spelling brought a slight smile to his lips, but he quickly
turned it off, for despite the atrociousness of it, PugAlNash
nevertheless was one score up on him. For Pug had been able,
after a fashion, to master the language of Earth, while he had
bogged down completely when confronted with Pug's language.

I profetick and wach ahed for you.

It was crazy, he told himself. It was, perhaps, some sort of joke, the kind of thing that passed for a joke with Pug.

He put the note away and prowled the apartment restlessly, vaguely upset by the whole pile-up of worries.

What should he do about the Griffin offer?

Why had he shared the leaf with the Widow Foshay?

What about that crack of Pug's?

He went to the bookshelves and put out a finger and ran it along the massive set of *Galactic Abstracts*. He found the right volume and took it back to the desk with him.

He leafed through it until he found *Unuk al Hay*. Pug, he remembered, lived on Planet X of the system.

He wrinkled up his forehead as he puzzled out the meaning of the compact, condensed, sometimes cryptic wording, bristling with fantastic abbreviations. It was a bloated nuisance, but it made sense, of course. There was just too much information to cover in the galaxy—the set of books, unwieldy as it might be, would simply become unmanageable if anything like completeness of expression and description were attempted.

X—It.kn., int., uninh. hu., (T-67), tr. intrm. (T-102) med. hbs., leg. forst., diff. lang ...

Wait a second, there!
Leg. forst.
Could that be *legend of foresight*?
He read it again, translating as he went:

X—little known, intelligence, uninhabitable for humans (see table 67), trade by intermediaries (see table 102), medical herbs, legend (or legacy?) of foresight, difficult language ...

And that last one certainly was right. He'd gained a working knowledge of a lot of alien tongues, but with Pug's he could not even get an inkling.
Leg. forst.?
One couldn't be sure, but it could be—it could be!
He slapped the book shut and took it back to the shelf.
So you watch ahead for me, he said.
And why? To what purpose?
PugAlNash, he said, a little pleased, *some day I'll wring your scrawny, meddling neck.*

But, of course, he wouldn't. PugAlNash was too far away and he might not be scrawny and there was no reason to believe he even had a neck.

When bedtime came around, he got into his flame-red pajamas with the yellow parrots on them and sat on the edge of the bed, wiggling his toes.

It had been quite a day, he thought.

He'd have to talk with Tony about this Government offer to sell him the stamp material. Perhaps, he thought, he should insist upon it even if it meant a loss of possible revenue to Efficiency, Inc. He might as well get what he could and what he wanted when it was for the taking. For Tony, before they were through with it, probably would beat him out of what he had coming to him. He had expected it by now—but more than likely Tony had been too busy to indulge in any crookedness. Although it was a wonder, for Tony enjoyed a dishonest dollar twice as much as he did an honest one.

He remembered that he had told Griffin that he had faith in Tony and he guessed that he'd been right—he had faith in him and a little pride as well. Tony was an unprincipled rascal and there was no denying it. Thinking about it, Packer chuckled fondly. *Just like me,* he told himself, *when I was young as Tony and was still in business.*

There had been that triple deal with the bogus Chippendale and the Antarian paintings and the local version of moonshine from out in the Packrat system. *By God,* he told himself, *I skinned all three of them on that one.*

The phone rang and he padded out of the bedroom, his bare feet slapping on the floor.

The phone kept on insisting.

"All right!" yelled Packer angrily. "I'm coming!"

He reached the desk and picked up the phone.

"This is Pickering," said the voice.

"Pickering. Oh, sure. Glad to hear from you."

"The man you talked with about the Polaris cover."

"Yes, Pickering. I remember you."

"I wonder, did you ever find that cover?"

"Yes, I found it. Sorry, but the strip had only four. I told you five, I fear. An awful memory, but you know how it goes. A man gets old and—"

"Mr. Packer, will you sell that cover?"

"Sell it? Yes, I guess I told you that I would. Man of my word, you realize, although I regret it now."

"It's a fine one, then?"

"Mr. Pickering," said Packer, "considering that it's the only one in existence—"

"Could I come over to see it sometime soon?"

"Any time you wish. Any time at all."

"You will hold it for me?"

"Certainly," consented Packer. "After all, no one knows as yet that I have the thing."

"And the price?"

"Well, now, I told you a quarter million, but I was talking then about a strip of five. Since it's only four, I'd be willing to shave it some. I'm a reasonable man, Mr. Pickering. Not difficult to deal with."

"I can see you aren't," said Pickering with a trace of bitterness.

They said good night and Packer sat in the chair and put his bare feet up on the desk and wiggled his toes, watching them with a certain fascination, as if he had never seen them before.

He'd sell Pickering the four-strip cover for two hundred thousand. Then he'd let it get noised about that there was a five-strip cover, and once he heard that, Pickering would be beside himself and frothing at the mouth. He'd be afraid that someone might get ahead of him and buy the five-stamp strip while he had only four. And that would be a public humiliation that a collector of Pickering's stripe simply couldn't stand.

Packer chortled softly to himself.

"Bait," he said aloud.

He probably could get half a million out of that five-strip piece. He'd make Pickering pay for it. He'd have to start it high, of course, and let Pickering beat him down.

He looked at the clock upon the desk and it was ten o'clock—a good hour past his usual bedtime.

He wiggled his toes some more and watched them. Funny thing about it, he wasn't even sleepy. He didn't want to go to bed; he'd got undressed from simple force of habit.

Nine o'clock, he thought, is a hell of a time for a man to go to bed. He could remember a time when he had never turned in until well after midnight and there had been many certain

81

memorable occasions, he chucklingly recalled, when he'd not gone to bed at all.

But there had been something to do in those days. There had been places to go and people to meet and food had tasted proper and the liquor had been something a man looked forward to. They didn't make decent liquor these days, he told himself. And there were no great cooks any more. And no entertainment, none worthy of the name. All his friends had either died or scattered; none of them had lasted.

Nothing lasts, he thought.

He sat wiggling his toes and looking at the clock and somehow he was beginning to feel just a bit excited, although he could not imagine why.

In the silence of the room there were two sounds only—the soft ticking of the clock and the syrupy gurgling of the basket full of spores.

He leaned around the corner of the desk and looked at the basket and it was there, four-square and solid—a basketful of fantasy come to sudden and enduring life.

Someday, he thought, someone would find where the spores came from—what distant planet in what misty reaches out toward the rim of the thinning galaxy. Perhaps even now the origin of the stamps could be determined if he'd only release the data that he had, if he would show the covers with the yellow stamps to some authority. But the covers and the data were a trade secret and had become too valuable to be shown to anyone; they were tucked away deep inside a bank vault.

Intelligent spores, he mused—what a perfect medium for the carrying of the mail. You put a dab of them on a letter or a package and you told them, somehow or other, where the letter or the package was to go and they would take it there. And once the job was done, then the spores encysted until the day that someone else, or something else, should recall them to their labors.

And today they were laboring for the Earth and the day would come, perhaps, when they'd be housekeepers to the entire Earth. They'd run all business efficiently and keep all homes picked up and neat; they would clean the streets and keep them free of litter and introduce everywhere an era of such order and such cleanliness as no race had ever known.

He wiggled his toes and looked at the clock again. It was not ten-thirty yet and it was really early. Perhaps he should change his mind—perhaps he should dress again and go for a moonlight stroll. For there was a moon; he could see it through the window.

Damn old fool, he told himself, whuffling out his whiskers.

But he took his feet down off the desk and paddled toward the bedroom.

He chuckled as he went, planning exactly how he was going to skin Pickering to within an inch of that collector's parsimonious life.

He was bending at the mirror, trying to make his tie track, when the doorbell set up a clamor.

If it was Pickering, he thought, he'd throw the damn fool out. Imagine turning up at this time of night to do a piece of business that could better wait till morning.

It wasn't Pickering.

The man's card said he was W. Frederick Hazlitt and that he was president of the Hazlitt Suppliers Corporation.

"Well, Mr. Hazlitt?"

"I'd like to talk to you a minute," Hazlitt said, peering furtively around. "You're sure that we're alone here?"

"Quite alone," said Packer.

"This is a matter of some delicacy," Hazlitt told him, "and of some alarm as well. I came to you rather than Mr. Anton Camper because I know of you by reputation as a man of proven business sagacity. I feel you could understand the problem where Mr. Camper—"

"Fire away," invited Packer cordially.

He had a feeling that he was going to enjoy this. The man was obviously upset and scared to death as well.

Hazlitt hunched forward in his chair and his voice dropped almost to a whisper.

"Mr. Packer," he confided in stricken horror, "I am becoming honest!"

"That's too bad," said Packer sympathetically.

"Yes, it is," said Hazlitt soberly. "A man in my position—in any business connection—simply can't be honest. Mr. Packer, I'll tell you confidentially that I lost out on one of the biggest deals in all my business life just last week because I had grown honest."

"Maybe," Packer suggested, "if you persevered, if you set your heart on it, you could remain at least partially dishonest."

Hazlitt shook his head dolefully. "I tell you, sir, I can't. I've tried. You don't know how hard I've tried. And no matter how I try, I find myself telling the truth about everything. I find that I cannot take unfair advantage of anyone, not even of a customer. I even found myself the other day engaged in cutting my profit margins down to a more realistic figure—"

"Why, that's horrible!" cried Packer.

"And it's all your fault," yelled Hazlitt.

"My fault," protested Packer, whuffling out his whiskers. "Upon my word, Mr Hazlitt, I can't see how you can say a thing like that. I haven't had a thing to do with it."

"It's your Efficiency units," howled Hazlitt. "They're the cause of it."

"The Efficiency units have nothing to do with you," declared Packer angrily. "All they do . . ."

He stopped.

Good Lord, he thought, they could!

He'd been feeling better than he'd felt for years and he didn't need his nap of an afternoon and here he was, dressing to go out in the middle of the night!

"How long has this been going on?" he asked in growing horror.

"For a month at least," said Hazlitt. "I think I first noticed it a month or six weeks ago."

"Why didn't you simply heave the unit out?"

"I did," yelled Hazlitt, "but it did no good."

"I don't understand. If you threw it out that should be the end of it."

"That's what I thought at the time, myself. But I was wrong. That yellow stuff's still there. It's growing in the cracks and floating in the air and you can't get rid of it. Once you have it, you are stuck with it."

Packer clucked in sympathy.

"You could move, perhaps."

"Do you realize what that would cost me, Packer? And besides, as far as I'm concerned, it simply is no good. The stuff's inside of me!"

He pounded at his chest. "I can feel it here, inside of me—turning me honest, making a good man out of me,

84

making me orderly and efficient, just like it made our files. And I don't want to be a good man, Packer—I want to make a lot of money!"

"There's one consolation," Packer told him. "Whatever is happening to you undoubtedly also is happening to your competitors."

"But even if that were the case," protested Hazlitt, "it would be no fun. What do you think a man goes into business for? To render service, to become identified with the commercial community, to make money only? No, sir, I tell you—it's the thrill of skinning a competitor, of running the risk of losing your own shirt, of—"

"Amen," Packer said loudly.

Hazlitt stared at him. "You, too . . ."

"Not a chance," said Packer proudly. "I'm every bit as big a rascal as I ever was."

Hazlitt settled back into his chair. His voice took on an edge, grew a trifle cold.

"I had considered exposing you, warning the world, and then I saw I couldn't. . . ."

"Of course you can't," said Packer gruffly. "You don't enjoy being laughed at. You are the kind of man who can't stand the thought of being laughed at."

"What's your game, Packer?"

"My game?"

"You introduced the stuff. You must have known what it would do. And yet you say you are unaffected by it. What are you shooting at—gobbling up the entire planet?"

Packer whuffled. "I hadn't thought of it," he said. "But it's a capital idea."

He rose stiffly to his feet. "Little old for it," he said, "but I have a few years yet. And I'm in the best of fettle. Haven't felt—"

"You were going out," said Hazlitt, rising. "I'll not detain you."

"I thank you, sir," said Packer. "I noticed that there was a moon and I was going for a stroll. You wouldn't join me, would you?"

"I have more important things to do, Packer, than strolling in the moonlight."

"I have no doubt of that," said Packer, bowing slightly.

"You would, of course, an upright, honest businessman like you."

Hazlitt slammed the door as he went out.

Packer padded back to the bedroom, took up the tie again.

Hazlitt an honest man, he thought. And how many other honest men this night? And a year from now—how many honest men in the whole wide world just one year from now? How long before the entire Earth would be an honest Earth? With spores lurking in the cracks and floating in the air and running with the rivers, it might not take so long.

Maybe that was the reason Tony hadn't skinned him yet. Maybe Tony was getting honest, too. Too bad, thought Packer, gravely. Tony wouldn't be half as interesting if he should happen to turn honest.

And the Government? A Government that had come begging for the spores—begging to be honest, although to be completely fair one must admit the Government as yet did not know about the honesty.

That was a hot one, Packer told himself. An honest Government! And it would serve those stinkers right! He could see the looks upon their faces.

He gave up the business of the tie and sat down on the bed and shook for minutes with rumbling belly laughter.

At last he wiped the tears out of his eyes and finished with the tie.

Tomorrow morning, bright and early, he'd get in touch with Griffin and arrange the package deal for the stamp material. He'd act greedy and drive a hard bargain and then, in the end, pay a bit more than the price agreed upon for a long-term arrangement. An honest Government, he told himself, would be too honest to rescind such an agreement even if, in the light of its new honesty, it should realize the wrongness of it. For, happily, one of the tenets of honesty was to stay stuck with a bad bargain, no matter how arrived at.

He shucked into his jacket and went into the living room. He stopped at the desk and opened the drawer. Reaching in, he lifted the lid of the box of leaf. He took a pinch and had it halfway to his mouth when the thought struck him suddenly and he stood for a moment frozen while all the gears came together, meshing, and the pieces fell into a pattern and he knew, without even asking, why he was the only genuine dishonest man left on the entire Earth.

I profetick and wach ahed for you!

He put the leaf into his mouth and felt the comfort of it.

Antidote, he thought, and knew that he was right.

But how could Pug have known—how could he have foreseen the long, twisting tangle of many circumstances which must inevitably crystallize into this very moment?

Leg. forst.?

He closed the lid of the box and shut the drawer and turned toward the door.

The only dishonest man in the world, he thought. Immune to the honesty factor in the yellow spores because of the resistance built up within him by his long use of the leaf.

He had set a trap tonight to victimize Pickering and tomorrow he'd go out and fox the Government and there was no telling where he'd go from there. Hazlitt had said something about taking over the entire planet and the idea was not a bad one if he could only squeeze out the necessary time.

He chuckled at the thought of how all the honest suckers would stand innocently in line, unable to do a thing about it—all fair prey to the one dishonest man in the entire world. A wolf among the sheep!

He drew himself erect and pulled the white gloves on carefully. He flicked his walking stick. Then he thumped himself on the chest—just once—and let himself out into the hall. He did not bother to lock the door behind him.

In the lobby, as he stepped out of the elevator, he saw the Widow Foshay coming in the door. She turned and called back cheerfully to friends who had brought her home.

He lifted his hat to her with an olden courtesy that he thought he had forgotten.

She threw up her hands in mock surprise. "Mr. Packer," she cried, "what has come over you? Where do you think you're going at this time of night, when all honest people are abed?"

"Minerva," he told her gravely, "I was about to take a stroll. I wonder if you might come along with me?"

She hesitated for an instant, just long enough to give the desired small show of reluctance and indecision.

He whuffled out his moustache at her. "Besides," he said, "I am not an honest person."

He offered her his arm with distinguished gallantry.

SO BRIGHT THE VISION

The showroom was in the decorous part of town, where Kemp Hart seldom found himself. It was a long way from his usual haunts and he was surprised to find that he had walked so far. In fact, he would not have walked at all if his credit had been good at the Bright Star bar where his crowd hung out.

As soon as he realized where he was he knew he should turn around and walk rapidly away, for he was out of place in this district of swank publishers, gold-plated warrens and famous eateries. But the showroom held him. It would not let him go. He stood in front of it in all his down-at-the-heels unkemptness, one hand thrust in a pocket, fugitively rubbing between thumb and finger the two small coins that still remained to him.

Behind the glass the machines were shining-wonderful, the sort of merchandise that belonged on this svelte and perfumed street. One machine in the corner of the showroom was bigger and shinier than the others and had about it a rare glint of competence. It had a massive keyboard for the feeding in of data and it had a hundred slots or so for the working tapes and films. It had a mood control calibrated more sensitively than any he had ever seen and in all probability a lot of other features that were not immediately apparent.

With a machine such as that, Hart told himself, a man could become famous almost automatically and virtually overnight. He could write anything he wished and he would write it well and the doors of the most snooty of the publishers would stand open to him.

But much as he might wish to, there was no use of going in to see it. There was nothing to be gained by even thinking about it. It was just something he could stand and look at from beyond the showroom's glass.

And yet, he told himself, he had a perfect right to go in and look it over. There was not a thing to stop him. Nothing, at least, beyond the sneer upon the salesman's face at the sight of him—the silent, polite, well-disciplined contempt when he turned and slunk away.

He looked furtively up and down the street and the street was empty. The hour was far too early for this particular street to have come to life, and it occurred to him that if he just walked in and asked to see the machine, it would be all right. Perhaps he could explain he did not wish to buy it, but just to look at it. Maybe if he did that they wouldn't sneer at him. Certainly no one could object. There must be a lot of people, even rich and famous people, who only come to look.

He edged along the showroom, studying the machines and heading for the door, telling himself that he would not go in, that it was foolish to go in, but secretly knowing that he would.

He reached the door and opened it and stepped inside. The salesman appeared almost as if by magic.

"The yarner in the corner," Hart said. "I wonder if I might—"

"Most certainly," said the salesman. "If you'll just come along with me."

In the corner of the showroom, the salesman draped his arm across the machine affectionately.

"It is our newest model," he said. "We call it the Classic, because it has been designed and engineered with but one thought in mind—the production of the classic. It is, we think, a vast improvement over our Best Seller Model, which, after all, is intended to turn out no better than best sellers—even though on occasion it has turned out certain minor classics. To be quite honest with you, sir, I would suspect that in almost every one of those instances, it had been souped up a bit. I am told some people are very clever that way."

Hart shook his head. "Not me. I'm all thumbs when it comes to tinkering."

"In that case," said the salesman, "the thing for you to do is buy the best yarner that you can. Used intelligently, there's virtually no limit to its versatility. And in this particular model the quality factor is much higher than in any of the others. Although naturally, to get the best results you must be selective in your character films and your narrative problem tapes. But that needn't worry you. We have a large stock of tapes and films and some new mood and atmosphere fixers that are quite unique. They come fairly high, of course, but—"

"By the way, just what is the price of this model?"

"It's only twenty-five thousand," the salesman told him, brightly. "Don't you wonder, sir, how it can be offered at so ridiculous a figure? The engineering that went into it is remarkable. We worked on it for ten full years before we were satisfied. And during those ten years the specifications were junked and redrawn time and time again to keep pace with our developmental research."

He slapped the shiny machine with a jubilant hand.

"I can guarantee you, sir, but that nowhere can you get a product superior to this. It has everything. Millions of probability factors have been built into it, assuring you of sure-fire originality. No danger of stumbling into the stereotype, which is not true at all with so many of the cheaper models. The narrative bank alone is capable of turning out an almost infinite number of situations on any particular theme and the character developer has thousands of points of reference instead of the hundred or so you find in inferior models. The semantics section is highly selective and sensitive and you must not overlook—"

"It's a good machine," interposed Hart. "But it costs a bit too much. Now, if you had something else . . ."

"Most certainly, sir. We have many other models."

"Would you take a machine in trade?"

"Gladly. What kind of machine do you have, sir?"

"An Auto-Author Ninety-six."

The salesman froze just slightly. He shook his head, half sadly, half in bewilderment. "Well, now, I don't know if we could allow you much for that. It's a fairly old type of machine. Almost obsolete."

"But you could give me something?"

"I think so. Not a great deal, though."

"And time payment?"

"Yes, certainly. We could work something out. If you would give me your name."

Hart told him what it was.

The salesman jotted it down and said, "Excuse me a moment, sir."

Hart stood for a moment, looking after him. Then, like a sneak thief in the night, he moved softly to the front door and walked swiftly down the street.

There was no use in staying. No use at all of waiting for the salesman to come back and shake his hand and say, "We're very sorry, sir."

We're very sorry, sir, because we've looked up your credit rating and it's absolutely worthless. We checked your sales record and found you sold just one short story in the last six months.

"It was a mistake to go for a walk at all," Hart told himself, not without bitterness.

Downtown, in a section of the city far removed from the glamorous showroom, Hart climbed six flights of stairs because the elevator was out of whack again.

Behind the door that said Irving Publications, the pre-occupied receptionist stopped filing her nails long enough to make a motion with her thumb toward the inner office.

"Go on in and see him," she said.

Ben Irving sat behind a heaped-up desk cluttered with manuscripts, proofs and layout sheets. His sleeves were rolled up to his elbows and he wore an eyeshade. He always wore the eyeshade and that was one of the minor mysteries of the place, for at no time during the day was there light enough in his dingy office to blind a self-respecting bat.

He looked up and blinked at Hart.

"Glad to see you, Kemp," he said. "Sit down. What's on you mind today?"

Hart took a chair. "I was wondering. About that last story that I sent you—"

"Haven't got around to it yet," said Irving. He waved his hand at the mess upon his desk by way of explanation.

"Mary!" he shouted.

The receptionist stuck her head inside the door.

"Get Hart's manuscript," he said, "and let Millie have a look at it."

Irving leaned back in his chair. "This won't take long," he said. "Millie's a fast reader."

"I'll wait," said Hart.

"I've got something for you," Irving told him. "We're starting a new magazine, aimed at the tribes out in the Algol system. They're a primitive sort of people, but they can read, Lord love them. We had the devil's own time finding someone

91

who could do the translations for us and it'll cost more than we like to pay to have the type set up. They got the damnedest alphabet you ever saw. We finally found a printer who had some in his fonts."

"What kind of stuff?" Hart asked.

"Simple humanoid," Irving replied. "Blood and thunder and a lot of spectacle. Life is tough and hard out there, so we have to give them something with plenty of color in it that's easy to read. Nothing fancy, mind you."

"Sounds all right."

"Good basic hack," said Irving. "See how it goes out there and if it goes all right we'll make translations for some of the primitive groups out in the Capella region. Minor changes, maybe, but none too serious."

He squinted meditatively at Hart.

"Not too much pay. But if it goes over we'll want a lot of it."

"I'll see what I can do," said Hart. "Any taboos? Anything to duck?"

"No religion at all," the editor told him. "They've got it, of course, but it's so complicated that you'd better steer clear of it entirely. No mushy stuff. Love don't rate with them. They buy their women and don't fool around with love. Treasure and greed would be good. Any standard reference word will give you a line on that. Fantastic weapons—the more gruesome the better. Bloodshed, lots of it. Hatred, that's their dish. Hatred and vengeance and hell-for-leather living. And you simply got to keep it moving."

"I'll see what I can do."

"That's the second time you've said that."

"I'm not doing so good, Ben. Once I could have told you *yes*. Once I could have hauled it over by the ton."

"Lost the touch?"

"Not the touch. The machine. My yarner is haywire. I might just as well try to write my stories by hand."

Irving shuddered at the thought.

"Fix it up," he said. "Tinker with it."

"I'm no good at that. Anyhow, it's too old. Almost obsolete."

"Well, do the best you can. I'd like to go on buying from you."

The girl came in. Without looking at Hart she laid the manuscript down upon the desk. From where he sat, Hart could see the single word the machine had stamped upon its face: REJECTED.

"Emphatic," said the girl. "Millie almost stripped a gear."

Irving pitched the manuscript to Hart.

"Sorry, Kemp. Better luck next time."

Hart rose, holding the manuscript in his hand. "I'll try this other thing," he said.

He started for the door.

"Just a minute," Irving said, his voice sympathetic.

Hart turned back.

Irving brought out his billfold, stripped out two tens and held them out.

"No," said Hart, staring at the bills longingly.

"It's a loan," said the editor. "Damn it, man, you can take a loan. You'll be bringing me some stuff."

"Thanks, Ben. I'll remember this."

He stuffed the bills into his pocket and made a swift retreat.

Bitter dust burned in his throat and there was a hard, cold lump in the center of his belly.

Got something for you, Ben had said. *Good basic hack.*

Good basic hack.

So that was what he'd sunk to!

Angela Maret was the only patron in the Bright Star bar when Hart finally arrived there, with money in his pocket and a man-sized hankering for a glass of beer. Angela was drinking a weird sort of pink concoction that looked positively poisonous. She had her glasses on and her hair skinned back and was quite obviously on a literary binge. It was a shame, Hart thought. She could be attractive, but preferred not to be.

The instant Hart joined her Blake, the bartender, came over to the table and just stood there, with his fists firmly planted on his hips.

"Glass of beer," Hart told him.

"No more cuff," Blake said, with an accusing stare.

"Who said anything about cuff? I'll pay for it."

Blake scowled. "Since you're loaded, how about paying on the bill?"

"I haven't got that kind of money. Do I get the beer or don't I?"

Watching Blake waddle back to the bar, Hart was glad he had had the foresight to stop and buy a pack of cigarettes to break one of the tens. Flash a ten and Blake would be on it in a second and have it chalked against his bill.

"Staked?" Angela asked sweetly.

"An advance," Hart told her, lying like a gentleman. "Irving has some stuff for me to do. He'll need a lot of it. It doesn't pay too well, of course."

Blake came with the beers and plunked it down on the table and waited pointedly for Hart to do the expected thing.

Hart paid him and he waddled off.

"Have you heard about Jasper?" Angela asked.

Hart shook his head. "Nothing recent," he said. "Did he finish his book?"

Angela's face lit up. "He's going on vacation. Can you imagine that? *Him* going on vacation!"

"I don't see why not," Hart protested. "Jasper has been selling. He's the only one of us who manages to stay loaded week after week."

"But that's not it, Kemp. Wait until I tell you—it simply is a scream. Jasper thinks he can write better if he goes off on vacation."

"Well, why not? Just last year Don went to one of those summer camps. That Bread Loaf thing, as they call it."

"All they do there," she said, "is brush up on mechanics. It's a sort of refresher course on the gadgetry of yarners. How to soup up the old heap so it'll turn out fresher stuff."

"I still don't see why Jasper can't take a vacation if he can afford it."

"You're so dense," said Angela. "Don't you get the point at all?"

"I get the point all right. Jasper thinks there's still a human factor in our writing. He's not entirely satisfied to get his facts out of a standard reference work or encyclopedia. He's not content to let the yarner define an emotion he has never felt or the color of a sunset he has never seen. He was nuts enough to hint at that and you and the rest of them have been riding him. No wonder the guy is eccentric. No wonder he keeps his door locked all the time."

"That locked door," Angela said cattily, "is symbolic of the kind of man he is."

"I'd lock my door," Hart told her. "I'd be eccentric too—if I could turn it out like Jasper. I'd walk on my hands. I'd wear a sarong. I'd even paint my face bright blue."

"You sound like you believe the same as Jasper does."

He shook his head. "No, I don't think the way he does. I know better. But if he wants to think that way let him go ahead and think it."

"You do," she crowed at him. "I can see it in your face. You think it's possible to be independently creative."

"No, I don't. I know it's the machines that do the creating— not us. We're nothing but attic tinkers. We're literary mechanics. And I suppose that's the way it should be. There is, naturally, the yearning for the past. That's been evident in every age. The 'good old days' complex. Back in those days a work of fiction was writ by hand and human agony."

"The agony's still with us, Kemp."

He said, "Jasper's a mechanic. That's what's wrong with me. I can't even repair that junk-heap of mine and you should see the way Jasper has his clunk souped up."

"You could hire someone to repair it. There are firms that do excellent work."

"I never have the money."

He finished his beer.

"What's that stuff you're drinking?" he asked. "Want another one?"

She pushed her glass away. "I don't like that mess," she said. "I'll have a beer with you if you don't mind."

Hart signaled to Blake for two beers.

"What are you doing now, Angela?" he asked. "Still working on the book?"

"Working up some films," she said.

"That's what I'll have to do this afternoon. I need a central character for this Irving stuff. Big and tough and boisterous— but not too uncouth. I'll look along the riverfront."

"They come high now, Kemp," she said. "Even those crummy aliens are getting wise to us. Even the ones from *way out*. I paid twenty for one just the other day and he wasn't too hot, either."

"It's cheaper than buying made-up films."

"Yes, I agree with you there. But it's a lot more work."

Blake brought the beer and Hart counted out the change into his waiting palm.

"Get some of this new film," Angela advised. "It's got the old stuff beat forty different ways. The delineation is sharper and you catch more of the marginal factors. You get a more rounded picture of the character. You pick up all the nuances of the subject, so to speak. It makes your people more believable. I've been using it."

"It comes high, I suppose," he said.

"Yes, it's a bit expensive," she admitted.

"I've got a few spools of the old stuff. I'll have to get along with that."

"I've an extra fifty you can have."

He shook his head. "Thanks, Angela. I'll cadge drinks and bum meals and hit up for a cigarette, but I'm not taking a fifty you'll need yourself. There's none of us so solvent we can lend someone else a fifty."

"Well, I would have done so gladly. If you should change your mind—"

"Want another beer?" Hart asked, cutting her short.

"I have to get to work."

"So have I," said Hart.

Hart climbed the stairs to the seventh floor, then went down the corridor and knocked on Jasper Hansen's door.

"Just a minute," said a voice from within the room.

He waited for three minutes. Finally a key grated in the lock and the door was opened wide.

"Sorry I took so long," apologized Jasper. "I was setting up some data and I couldn't quit. Had to finish it."

Hart nodded. Jasper's explanation was understandable. It was difficult to quit in the middle of setting up some data that had taken hours to assemble.

The room was small and littered. In one corner stood the yarner, a shining thing, but not as shiny as the one he'd seen that morning in the uptown showroom. A typewriter stood on a littered desk, half covered by the litter. A long shelf sagged with the weight of dog-eared reference works. Bright-jacketed books were piled helter-skelter in a corner. A cat slept on an unmade bed. A bottle of liquor stood on a cupboard beside a loaf of bread. Dirty dishes were piled high in the sink.

"Heard you're going on vacation, Jasper," Hart said.

Jasper gave him a wary look. "Yes, I thought I might."

"I was wondering, Jasper, if you'd do something for me."

"Just name it."

"When you're gone, could I use your yarner?"

"Well, now, I don't know, Kemp. You see—"

"Mine is busted and I haven't the cash to fix it. But I've got a line on something. If you'd let me use yours, I could turn out enough in a week or two to cover the repair bill."

"Well, now," said Jasper, "you know I'd do anything for you. Anything at all. But that yarner—I just can't let you use it. I got it jiggered up. There isn't a circuit in it that has remained the way it was originally. There isn't a soul but myself who could operate it. If someone else tried to operate it they might burn it out or kill themselves or something."

"You could show me, couldn't you?" Hart asked, almost pleadingly.

"It's far too complicated. I've tinkered with it for years," said Jasper.

Hart managed a feeble grin. "I'm sorry, I thought—"

Jasper draped an arm around his shoulder. "Anything else. Just ask me anything."

"Thanks," said Hart, turning to go.

"Drink?"

"No, thanks," said Hart, and walked out of the door.

He climbed two more flights to the topmost floor and went into his room. His door was never locked. There was nothing in it for anyone to steal. And for that matter, he wondered, what did Jasper have that anyone might want?

He sat down in a rickety chair and stared at his yarner. It was old and battered and ornery, and he hated it.

It was worthless, absolutely worthless, and yet he knew he would have to work with it. It was all he had. He'd slave and reason with it and kick it and swear at it and he'd spend sleepless nights with it. And gurgling and clucking with overweaning gratitude, it would turn out endless reams of mediocrity that no one would buy.

He got up, and walked to the window. Far below lay the river and at the wharfs a dozen ships were moored, disgorging rolls of paper to feed the hungry presses that thundered day and night. Across the river a spaceship was rising from the spaceport, with the faint blue flicker of the ion stream wisping from the tubes. He watched it until it was out of sight.

There were other ships, with their noses pointed at the sky, waiting for the signal—the punched button, the flipped switch, the flicker of a piece of navigation tape—that would send them hounding homeward. First out into the blackness and then into that other place of weird other-worldness that annihilated time and space, setting at defiance the theoretic limit of the speed of light. Ships from many stars, all come to Earth for one thing only, for the one commodity that Earthmen had to sell.

He pulled his eyes from the fascination of the spaceport and looked across the sprawling city, the tumbled, canted, box-like rectangles of the district where he lived, while far to the north shone the faery towers and the massive greatness of the famous and the wise.

A fantastic world, he thought. A fantastic world to live in. Not the kind of world that H. G. Wells and Stapledon had dreamed. With them it had been a far wandering and galactic empire, a glory and a greatness that Earth had somehow missed when the doors to space had finally been opened. Not the thunder of the rocket, but the thunder of the press. Not the great and lofty purpose, but the faint, quiet, persistent voice spinning out a yarn. Not the far sweep of new planets, but the attic room and the driving fear that the machine would fail you, that the tapes had been used too often, that the data was all wrong.

He went to the desk and pulled all three of the drawers. He found the camera in the bottom one beneath a pile of junk. He hunted for and found the film in the middle drawer, wrapped in aluminum foil.

Rough and tough, he thought, and it shouldn't be too hard to find a man like that in one of the dives along the riverfront, where the space crews on planet leave squandered their pay checks.

The first dive he entered was oppressive with the stink of a group of spidery creatures from Spica and he didn't stay. He grimaced distastefully and got out as fast as he could. The second was repellently patronized by a few cat-like denizens of Dahib and they were not what he was looking for.

But in the third he hit the jackpot, a dozen burly humanoids from Caph—great brawling creatures with a flair for extravagance in dress, a swashbuckling attitude and a prodigious appetite for lusty living. They were grouped about a large round table out in the center of the room and they were whooping it up. They were pounding the table with their tankards and chivvying the scuttling proprietor about and breaking into songs that they repeatedly interrupted with loud talk and argument.

Hart slipped into an unoccupied booth and watched the Caphians celebrate. One of them, bigger and louder and rowdier than the rest, wore red trousers, and a bright green shirt. Looped necklaces of platinum and outlandish alien gems encircled his throat and glittered on his chest, and his hair had not been trimmed for months. He wore a beard that was faintly satanic, and, startlingly enough, his ears were slightly pointed. He looked like an ugly customer to get into a fracas with. *And so*, thought Hart, *he's just the boy I want*.

The proprietor finally lumbered over to the booth.

"Beer," said Hart. "A big glass."

"Buster," said the man, "no one drinks beer here."

"Well, then, what have you got?"

"I got *bocca* and *igno* and *hzbut* and *greno* and—"

"*Bocca*," said Hart. He knew what *bocca* was and he didn't recognize any of the others. Lord knows what some of them might do to the human constitution. *Bocca*, at least, one could survive.

The man went away and in a little while came back with a mug of *bocca*. It was faintly greenish and it sizzled just a little. What was worse, it tasted like a very dilute solution of sulphuric acid.

Hart squeezed himself back into the corner of the booth and opened his camera case. He set the camera on the table, no farther forward than was necessary to catch Green Shirt in the lens. Sighting through the finder, he got the Caphian in focus, and then quickly pressed the button that set the instrument in motion.

Once that was done, he settled down to drinking *bocca*.

He sat there, gagging down the *bocca* and manipulating the camera. Fifteen minutes was all he needed. At the end of fifteen minutes Green Shirt would be on film. Probably not as good as if he had been using the new-fangled spools that Angela was using, but at least he'd have him.

The camera ground on, recording the Caphian's physical characteristics, his personal mannerisms, his habits of speech, his thought processes (if any), his way of life, his background, his theoretic reaction in the face of any circumstance.

Not three-dimensional, thought Hart, not too concise nor too distinctive, not digging deep into the character and analyzing him—but good enough for the kind of tripe he'd have to write for Irving.

Take this joker and surround him with a few other ruffians chosen haphazardly from the file. Use one of the films from the Deep Dark Villain reel, throw in an ingenious treasure situation and a glob of violence, dream up some God-awful background, and he'd have it, that is, if the yarner worked. . . .

Ten minutes gone. Just five more to go. In five more minutes he'd stop the camera, put it back into its case, slip the case into his pocket and get out of the place as fast as he could. Without causing undue notice, of course.

It had been simple, he thought—much simpler than he could possibly have imagined.

They're getting on to us, Angela had said. *Even these crummy aliens.*

Only three more minutes to go.

A hand came down from nowhere, and picked up the camera. Hart swiveled around. The proprietor stood directly behind him, with the camera under his arm.

Good Lord, thought Hart, *I was watching the Caphians so closely I forgot about this guy!*

The proprietor roared at him: "So! You sneak in here under false pretences to get your film! Are you trying to give my place a bad name?"

Swiftly Hart flung himself out of the booth, one frantic eye on the door. There was just a chance that he might make it. But the proprietor stuck out an expert foot and tripped him. Hart landed on his shoulders and somersaulted. He skidded across the floor, smashed into a table and rolled half under it.

The Caphians had come to their feet and were looking at him. He could see that they were hoping he'd get his head bashed in.

The proprietor hurled the camera with great violence to the floor. It came apart with an ugly, splintering sound. The film rolled free and snaked across the floor. The lens wobbled crazily. A spring came unloose from somewhere and went *zing*. It stood out at an angle, quivering.

Hart gathered his feet beneath him, and leaped out from the table. The Caphians started moving in on him—not rushing him, not threatening him in any way. They just kept walking toward him and spreading out so that he couldn't make a dash for the door.

He backed away, step by careful step, and the Caphians still continued their steady advance.

Suddenly he leaped straight toward them in a direct assault on the center of the line. He yelled and lowered his head and caught Green Shirt squarely in the belly. He felt the Caphian stagger and lurch to one side, and for a split second he thought that he had broken free.

But a hairy, muscular hand reached out and grabbed him and flung him to the floor. Someone kicked him. Someone stepped on his fingers. Someone else picked him up and threw him—straight through the open door into the street outside.

He landed on his back and skidded, with the breath completely knocked out of him. He came to rest with a jolt against the curbing opposite the place from which he had been heaved.

The Caphians, the full dozen of them, were grouped around the doorway, aroar with booming laughter. They slapped their thighs, and pounded one another on the back. They doubled over, shrieking. They shouted pleasantries and insults at him. Half of the jests he did not understand, but the ones that registered were enough to make his blood run cold.

He got up cautiously, and tested himself. He was considerably bruised and battered and his clothes were torn. But seemingly he had escaped any broken bones. He tried a few steps, limping. He tried to run and was surprised to find that he could.

Behind him the Caphians were still laughing. But there was no telling at what moment they might cease to think that his predicament was funny and start after him in earnest—for blood.

He raced down the street and ducked into an alley that led to a tangled square. He crossed the square into another street without pausing for breath and went running on. Finally he became satisfied that he was safe and sat down on a doorstep in an alley to regain his breath and carefully review the situation.

The situation, he realized, was bad. He not only had failed to get the character he needed; he had lost the camera, suffered a severe humiliation and barely escaped with his life.

There wasn't a thing that he could do about it. Actually, he told himself, he had been extremely lucky. For he didn't have a legal leg to stand on. He'd been entirely in the wrong. To film a character without the permission of the character's original was against the law.

It wasn't that he was a lawbreaker, he thought. It wasn't as if he'd deliberately set out to break the law. He'd been forced into it. Anyone who might have consented to serve as a character would have demanded money—more money than he was in a position to shell out.

But he did desperately need a character! He simply had to have one, or face utter defeat.

He saw that the sun had set, and that twilight was drifting in. The day, he thought, had been utterly wasted, and he had only himself to blame.

A passing police officer stopped and looked into the alley.

"You," he said to Hart. "What are you sitting there for?"

"Resting," Hart told him.

"All right. You're rested. Now get a move on."

Hart got a move on.

He was nearing home when he heard the crying in the areaway between an apartment house and a bindery. It was a funny sort of crying, a not-quite-human crying—perhaps not so much a crying as a sound of grief and loneliness.

He halted abruptly and stared around him. The crying had cut off, but soon it began again. It was a low and empty crying, a hopeless crying, a crying to one's self.

For a moment he stood undecided, then started to go on. But he had not gone three paces before he turned back. He stepped into the areaway and at the second step his foot touched something lying on the ground.

He squatted and looked at the form that lay there, crying to itself. It was a bundle—that described it best—a huddled, limp, sad bundle that moaned heartbrokenly.

He put a hand beneath it and lifted it and was surprised at

how little weight it had. Holding it firmly with one hand, he searched with the other for his lighter. He flicked the lighter and the flame was feeble, but he saw enough to make his stomach flop. It was an old blanket with a face that once had started out to be humanoid and then, for some reason, had been forced to change its mind. And that was all there was—a blanket and a face.

He thumbed the lighter down and crouched in the dark, his breath rasping in his throat. The creature was not only an alien. It was, even by alien standards, almost incredible. And how had an alien strayed so far from the spaceport? Aliens seldom wandered. They never had the time to wander, for the ships came in, freighted up with fiction, and almost immediately took off again. The crews stayed close to the rocket berths, seldom venturing farther than the dives along the riverfront.

He rose, holding the creature bundled across his chest as one would hold a child—it was not as heavy as a child—and feeling the infantlike warmth of it against his body and a strange companionship. He stood in the areaway while his mind went groping back in an effort to unmask the faint recognition he had felt. Somewhere, somehow, it seemed he once had heard or read of an alien such as this. But surely that was ridiculous, for aliens did not come, even the most fantastic of them, as a living blanket with the semblance of a face.

He stepped out into the street and looked down to examine the face again. But a portion of the creature's blanket-body had draped itself across its features and he could see only a waving blur.

Within two blocks he reached the Bright Star bar, went around the corner to the side door and started up the stairs. Footsteps were descending and he squeezed himself against the railing to let the other person past.

"Kemp," said Angela Maret. "Kemp, what have you there?"

"I found it in the street," Hart told her.

He shifted his arm a little and the blanket-body slipped and she saw the face. She moved back against the railing, her hand going to her mouth to choke off a scream.

"Kemp! How awful!"

"I think that it is sick. It—"

"What are you going to do?"

"I don't know," Hart said. "It was crying to itself. It was enough to break your heart. I couldn't leave it there."

"I'll get Doc Julliard."

Hart shook his head. "That wouldn't do any good. Doc doesn't know any alien medicine. Besides, he's probably drunk."

"No one knows any alien medicine," Angela reminded him. "Maybe we could get one of the specialists uptown." Her face clouded. "Doc is resourceful, though. He has to be down here. Maybe he could tell us—"

"All right," Hart said. "See if you can rout out Doc."

In his room he laid the alien on the bed. It was no longer whimpering. Its eyes were closed and it seemed to be asleep, although he could not be sure.

He sat on the edge of the bed and studied it and the more he looked at it the less sense it seemed to make. Now he could see how thin the blanket body was, how light and fragile. It amazed him that a thing so fragile could live at all, that it could contain in so inadequate a body the necessary physiological machinery to keep itself alive.

He wondered if it might be hungry and if so what kind of food it required. If it were really ill how could he hope to take care of it when he didn't know the first basic thing about it?

Maybe Doc— But no, Doc would know no more than he did. Doc was just like the rest of them, living hand to mouth, cadging drinks whenever he could get them, and practising medicine without adequate equipment and with a knowledge that had stopped dead in its tracks forty years before.

He heard footsteps coming up the stairs—light steps and trudging heavy ones. It had to be Angela with Doc. She had found him quickly and that probably meant he was sober enough to act and think with a reasonable degree of coordination.

Doc came into the room, followed by Angela. He put down his bag and looked at the creature on the bed.

"What have we here?" he asked and probably it was the first time in his entire career that the smug doctorish phrase made sense.

"Kemp found it in the street," said Angela quickly. "It's stopped crying now."

"Is this a joke?" Doc asked, half wrathfully. "If it is, young

104

man, I consider it in the worst possible taste."

Hart shook his head. "It's no joke. I thought that you might know—"

"Well, I don't," said Doc, with aggressive bitterness.

He let go of the blanket edge and it quickly flopped back upon the bed.

He paced up and down the room for a turn or two. Then he whirled angrily on Angela and Hart.

"I suppose you think that I should do something," he said. "I should at least go through the motions. I should act like a doctor. I'm sure that is what you're thinking. I should take its pulse and its temperature and look at its tongue and listen to its heart. Well, suppose you tell me how I do these things. Where do I find the pulse? If I could find it, what is its normal rate? And if I could figure out some way to take its temperature, what is the normal temperature for a monstrosity such as this? And if you would be so kind, would you tell me how— short of dissection—I could hope to locate the heart?"

He picked up his bag and started for the door.

"Anyone else, Doc?" Hart pleaded, in a conciliatory tone.

"Anyone who'd know?"

"I doubt it," Doc snapped.

"You mean there's *no one* who can do a thing? Is that what you're trying to say?"

"Look, son. Human doctors treat human beings, period. Why should we be expected to do more? How often are we called upon to treat an alien? We're not *expected* to treat aliens. Oh, possibly, once in a while some specialist or researcher may dabble in alien medicine. But that is the correct name for it—just plain dabbling. It takes years of a man's life to learn barely enough to qualify as a human doctor. How many lifetimes do you think we should devote to curing aliens?"

"All right, Doc. All right."

"And how can you even be sure there's something wrong with it?"

"Why, it was crying and I quite naturally thought—"

"It might have been lonesome or frightened or grieving. It might have been lost."

Doc turned to the door again.

"Thanks, Doc," Hart said.

"Not at all." The old man hesitated at the door. "You don't happen to have a dollar, do you? Somehow, I ran a little short."

"Here," said Hart, giving him a bill.

"I'll return it tomorrow," Doc promised.

He went clumping down the stairs.

Angela frowned. "You shouldn't have done that, Kemp. Now he'll get drunk and you'll be responsible."

"Not on a dollar," Hart said confidently.

"That's all you know about it. The kind of stuff Doc drinks—"

"Let him get drunk then. He deserves a little fun."

"But—" Angel motioned to the thing upon the bed.

"You heard what Doc said. He can't do anything. No one can do anything. When it wakes up—*if* it wakes up—it may be able to tell us what is wrong with it. But I'm not counting on that."

He walked over to the bed and stared down at the creature. It was repulsive and abhorrent and not in the least humanoid. But there was about it a pitiful loneliness and an incongruity that made a catch come to his throat.

"Maybe I should have left it in the areaway," he said. "I started to walk on. But when it began to cry again I went to it. Maybe I did wrong bothering with it at all. I haven't helped it any. If I'd left it there it might have turned out better. Some other aliens may be looking for it by now."

"You did right," said Angela. "Don't start in fighting with windmills."

She crossed the room and sat down in a chair. He went over to the window and stared somberly out across the city.

"What happened to you?" she asked.

"Nothing."

"But your clothes. Just look at your clothes."

"I got thrown out of a dive. I tried to take some film."

"Without paying for it."

"I didn't have the money."

"I offered you a fifty."

"I know you did. But I couldn't take it. Don't you understand, Angela? *I simply couldn't take it.*"

She said softly, "You're bad off, Kemp."

He swung around, outraged. She hadn't needed to say that. She had no right to say it. She—

106

He caught himself before the words came tumbling out.

She had a right. She'd offered him a fifty—but that had been only a part of it. She had the right to say it because she knew that she could say it. No one else in all the world could have felt the way she did about him.

"I can't write," he said. "Angela, no matter how I try, I can't make it come out right. The machine is haywire and the tapes are threadbare and most of them are patched."

"What have you had to eat today?"

"I had the beers with you and I had some *bocca*."

"That isn't eating. You wash your face and change into some different clothes and we'll go downstairs and get you some food."

"I have eating money."

"I know you have. You told me about the advance from Irving."

"It wasn't an advance."

"I know it wasn't, Kemp."

"What about the alien?"

"It'll be all right—at least long enough for you to get a bite to eat. You can't help it by standing here. You don't know how to help it."

"I guess you're right."

"Of course I am. Now get going and wash your dirty face. And don't forget your ears."

Jasper Hansen was alone in the Bright Star bar. They went over to his table and sat down. Jasper was finishing a dish of sauerkraut and pig's knuckles and was drinking wine with it, which seemed a bit blasphemous.

"Where's everyone else?" asked Angela.

"There's a party down the street," said Jasper. "Someone sold a book."

"Someone that we know?"

"Hell, no," Jasper said. "Just someone sold a book. You don't have to know a guy to go to his party when he sells a book."

"I didn't hear anything about it."

"Neither did the rest of the bunch. Someone looked in at the door and hollered about the party and everyone took off. Everyone but me. I can't monkey with no party. I've got work to do."

107

"Free food?" asked Angela.

"Yeah. Don't it beat you, though. Here we are, honorable and respected craftsmen, and every one of us will break a leg to grab himself a sandwich and a drink."

"Times are tough," said Hart.

"Not with me," said Jasper. "I keep working all the time."

"But work doesn't solve the main problem."

Jasper regarded him thoughtfully, tugging at his chin.

"What else is there?" he demanded. "Inspiration? Dedication? Genius? Go ahead and name it. We are mechanics, man. We got machines and tapes. We went into production two hundred years ago. We mechanized so we could go into top production so that people could turn out books and stories even if they had no talent at all. We got a job to do. We got to turn out tons of drivel for the whole damn galaxy. We got to keep them drooling over what is going to happen next to sloe-eyed Annie, queen of the far-flung spaceways. And we got to shoot up the lad with her and patch him up and shoot him up and patch him up and . . ."

He reached for an evening paper, opened it to a certain page and thumped his fist upon it.

"Did you see this?" he asked. "The Classic, they call it. Guaranteed to turn out nothing but a classic."

Hart snatched the paper from him and there it was, the wondrous yarner he had seen that morning, confronting him in all its glory from the center of a full-page.

"Pretty soon," said Jasper, "all you'll need to write is have a lot of money. You can go out and buy a machine like that and say turn out a story and press a button or flip a switch or maybe simply kick it and it'll cough out a story complete to the final exclamation point.

"It used to be that you could buy an old beat-up machine for, say, a hundred dollars and you could turn out any quantity of stuff—not good, but saleable. Today you got to have a high-priced machine and an expensive camera and a lot of special tape and film. Someday," he said, "the human race will outwit itself. Someday it will mechanize to the point where there won't be room for humans, but only for machines."

"You do all right," said Angela.

"That's because I keep dinging my machine up all the time. It don't give me no rest. That place of mine is half study and half machine shop and I know as much about electronics as I do about narration."

Blake came shuffling over.

"What'll it be?" he growled.

"I've eaten," Angela told him. "All I want is a glass of beer."

He turned to Hart. "How about you?" he demanded.

"Give me some of that stuff Jasper has—without the wine."

"No cuff," said Blake.

"Damn it, who said anything about cuff? Do you expect me to pay you before you bring it?"

"No," said Blake. "But immediately after I bring it."

He turned and shuffled off.

"Some day," said Jasper, "there has to be a limit to it. There must be a limit to it and we must be reaching it. You can only mechanize so far. You can assign only so many human activities and duties to intelligent machines. Who, two hundred years ago, would have said that the writing of fiction could have been reduced to a matter of mechanics?"

"Who, two hundred years ago," said Hart, "could have guessed that Earth could gear itself to a literary culture? But that is precisely what we have today. Sure, there are factories that build the machines we need and lumbermen who cut the trees for pulp and farmers who grow the food, and all the other trades and skills which are necessary to keep a culture operative. But by and large Earth today is principally devoted to the production of a solid stream of fiction for the alien trade."

"It all goes back to one peculiar trait," said Jasper. "A most unlikely trait to work—as it does—to our great advantage. We just happen to be the galaxy's only liars. In a mass of stars where truth is accepted as a universal constant, we are the one exception."

"You make it sound so horrible," protested Angela.

"I suppose I do, but that's the way it is. We could have become great traders and skinned all and sundry until they got wise to us. We could have turned our talent for the untruth into many different channels and maybe even avoided getting our heads bashed in. But instead we drifted into the one safe course. Our lying became an easy virtue. Now we can lie to our hearts' content and they lap it up. No one, nowhere, except right here on Earth, ever even tried to spin a yarn for simple entertainment, or to point a moral or for any other reason. They never attempted it because it would have been a lie, and we are the only liars in the universe of stars."

Blake brought the beer for Angela and the pig knuckles for Hart. Hart paid him out of hand.

"I've still got a quarter left," he said. "Have you any pie?"

"Apple."

"Here," said Hart, "I'll pay you in advance."

"First," went on Jasper, "it was told by mouth. Then it was writ by hand and now it's fabricated by machine. But surely that's not the end of it. There must be something else. There must be another way, a better way. There must be another step."

"I would settle for anything," said Hart. "Any way at all. I'd even write by hand if I thought I could go on selling."

"You can't!" Angela told him, sharply. "Why, it's positively indecent to even joke about it. You can say it as a joke just among the three of us, but if I ever hear you—"

Hart waved his hand. "Let it go. I'm sorry that I said it."

"Of course," said Jasper, "it's a great testimonial to the cleverness of Man, to the adaptability and resourcefulness of the human race. It is a somewhat ludicrous application of big business methods to what had always been considered a personal profession. But it works. Some day, I have no doubt, we may see the writing business run on production lines, with fiction factories running double shifts."

"No," Angela said. "No, you're wrong there, Jasper. Even with the mechanization, it's still the loneliest business on Earth."

"It is," agreed Jasper. "But I don't regret the loneliness part. Maybe I should, but I don't."

"It's a lousy way to make a living," said Angela, with a strange half-bitterness in her voice. "What are we contributing?"

"You are making people happy—if you can call some of our readers people. You are supplying entertainment."

"And the noble ideas?"

"There are even a few of those."

"It's more than that," said Hart. "More than entertainment, more than great ideas. It's the most innocent and the deadliest

110

propaganda in all of human history. The old writers, before the first space flight, glorified far wandering and galactic conquest and I think that they were justified. But they missed the most important development completely. They couldn't possibly foresee the way we would do it—with books, not battleships. We're softening up the galaxy with a constant stream of human thought. Our words are reaching farther than our spaceships ever could."

"That's the point I want to make," Jasper said, triumphantly. "You hit the point exactly. But if we are to tell the galaxy a story it must be a *human* story. If we sell them a bill of goods it must be a human bill of goods. And how can we keep it human if we relegate its telling to machines?"

"But they're human machines," objected Angela.

"A machine can't be purely human. Basically a machine is universal. It could be Caphian as well as human, or Aldebaran or Draconian or any other race. And that's not all. We let the machine set the norm. The one virtue of mechanics is that it sets a pattern. And a pattern is deadly in literary matters. It never changes. It keeps on using the same old limp plots in many different guises.

"Maybe at the moment it makes no difference to the races who are reading us, for as yet they have not developed anything approaching a critical faculty. But it should make some difference to us. It should make some difference in the light of a certain pride of workmanship we are supposed to have. And that is the trouble with machines. They are destroying the pride in us. Once writing was an art. But it is an art no longer. It's machine-produced, like a factory chair. A good chair, certainly. Good enough to sit on, but not a thing of beauty or of craftsmanship or—"

The door crashed open and feet pounded on the floor.

Just inside the door stood Green Shirt and behind him, grinning fiendishly, his band of Caphians.

Green Shirt advanced upon them happily, with his arms flung wide in greeting. He stopped beside Hart's chair and clapped a massive hand upon his shoulder.

"You recall me, don't you?" he asked in slow and careful English.

"Sure," Hart said, gulping. "Sure, I remember you. This is Miss Maret and over there is Mr. Hansen."

Green Shirt said, with precise bookishness, "So happy, I assure you."

"Have a seat," said Jasper.

"Glad to," said Green Shirt, hauling out a chair. His necklaces jingled musically as he sat down.

One of the other Caphians said something to him in a rapid-fire alien tongue. Green Shirt answered curtly and waved toward the door. The others marched outside.

"He is worried," Green Shirt said. "We will slow—how do you say it—we will slow the ship. They cannot leave without us. But I tell him not to worry. The captain will be glad we slow the ship when he see what we bring back."

He leaned forward and tapped Hart upon the knee.

"I look for you," he said. "I look high and wide."

"Who is this joker?" Jasper asked.

"Joker?" asked Green Shirt, frowning.

"A term of great respect," Hart hastily assured him.

"So," said Green Shirt. "You all write the stories?"

"Yes. All three of us."

"But *you* write them best.'

"I wouldn't say that exactly. You see—"

"You write the wild and woolly stories? The bang-bangs?"

"Yeah. I guess I'm guilty."

Green Shirt looked apologetic. "Had I known, we would not from the tavern have thrown you out. It was just big fun. We did not know you write the stories. When we find out who you are we try to catch you. But you run and hide."

"Just what is going on here, anyhow?" Angela demanded.

Green Shirt whooped for Blake.

"Set them up," he shouted. "These are my friends. Set up the best you have."

"The best I have," Blake said icily, "is Irish whiskey and that costs a buck a shot."

"I got the cash," said Green Shirt. "You get this name I cannot say, and you will get your cash."

He said to Hart, "I have a surprise for you, my friend. We love the writers of the bang-bangs. We read them *always*. We get much stimulation."

Jasper guffawed.

Green Shirt swung about in amazement, his bushy brows contracting.

112

"He's just happy," Hart explained, quickly. "He likes Irish whiskey."

"Fine," said Green Shirt, beaming. "You drink all you wish. I will give the cash. It is—how do you say—on me."

Blake brought the drinks and Green Shirt paid him.

"Bring the container," he said.

"The container?"

"He means the bottle."

"That'll be twenty dollars," said Blake.

"So," said Green Shirt, paying him.

They drank the whiskey and Green Shirt said to Hart, "My surprise is that you come with us."

"You mean in the ship?"

"We have never had a real live writer on our planet. You will have a good time. You will stay and write for us."

"Well," said Hart, "I'm not sure—"

"You try to take the picture. The tavern man explain it all to us. He say it is against the law. He say if I complain it will come big trouble."

"You can't do it, Kemp," protested Angela. "Don't let this big hyena bluff you. We'll pay your fine."

"We not complain," said Green Shirt gently. "We just with you mop up the condemned place."

Blake brought the bottle and thumped it down in the center of the table. Green Shirt picked it up and filled their glasses to the brim.

"Drink up," he said and set a fine example.

He drank and Green Shirt filled his glass again. Hart picked up his glass and twirled it in his fingers.

There had to be a way out of this mess, he told himself. It was absurd that this thundering barbarian from one of the farther suns should be able to walk into a bar and tell a man to come along with him.

However, there was no percentage in stirring up a fight—not with ten or eleven Caphians waiting just outside.

"I explain it to you," said Green Shirt. "I try hard to explain it well so that you will—so that you will—"

"Understand," supplied Jasper Hansen.

"I thank you, Hansen man. So you will understand. We get the stories only shortly ago. Many of the other races got them long ago, but with us it is new and most wonderful. It takes us—how would you say—out of ourselves. We get many things from other stars, useful things, things to hold in the hand, things to see and use. But from you we get the going of far places, the doing of great deeds, the thinking of great things."

He filled the glasses all around again.

"You understand?" Green Shirt asked.

They nodded.

"And now we go."

Hart rose slowly to his feet.

"Kemp, you can't!" screamed Angela.

"You shut the mouth," said Green Shirt.

Hart marched through the door and out into the street. The other Caphians oozed out of dark alleyways and surrounded him.

"Off we go," said Green Shirt, happily. "It gives big time on Caph."

Halfway to the river, Hart stopped in the middle of the street.

"I can't do it," he said.

"Can't do what?" asked Green Shirt, prodding him along.

"I let you think," said Hart, "that I was the man you wanted. I did it because I'd like to see your planet. But it isn't fair. I'm not the man you want."

"You write the bang-bangs, do you not? You think up the wild and woollies?"

"Certainly. But not really good ones. Mine aren't the kind where you hang on every word. There's another man who can do it better."

"This man we want," said Green Shirt. "Can you tell us where to find him?"

"That's easy. The other man at the table with us. The one who was so happy when you ordered whiskey."

"You mean the Hansen man?"

"He is the one, exactly."

"He write the bang-bangs good?"

"Much better than I do. He's a genius at it."

Green Shirt was overcome with gratitude. He hugged Hart to him in an extravagant expression of good will.

"You fair," he said. "You fine. It was nice of you to tell us."

A window banged up in a house across the street and a man stuck his head out.

"If you guys don't break it up," he bellowed, "I'll call the cops."

"We shatter the peace," sighed Green Shirt. "It is a queer law you have."

The window banged down again.

Green Shirt put a friendly hand upon Hart's shoulder. "We love the wild and woollies," he said gravely. "We want the very best. We thank you. We find this Hansen man."

He turned around and loped back up the street, followed by his ruffians.

Hart stood on the corner and watched them go. He drew a deep breath and let it slowly out.

It had been easy, he told himself, once you got the angle. And it had been Jasper, actually, who had given him the angle. *Truth is regarded as a universal constant,* Jasper had said. *We are the only liars.*

It had turned out tough on Jasper—a downright dirty trick. But the guy wanted to go on vacation, didn't he? And here was the prospect of a travel jaunt which would be really worthwhile. He'd refused the use of his machine and he had guffawed insultingly when Green Shirt had asked about the wild and woollies. If ever a guy had it coming to him, Jasper Hansen was that guy.

And above and beyond all that, he always kept his door locked—which showed a contemptible suspicion of his fellow writers.

Hart swung about and walked rapidly away in an opposite direction. Eventually he'd go back home, he told himself. But not right now. Later on he'd go, when the dust had settled slightly.

It was dawn when Hart climbed the stairs to the seventh floor and went down the corridor to Jasper Hansen's door. The door was locked as usual. But he took out of his pockets a thin piece of spring steel he'd picked up in a junkyard and did some judicious prying. In the matter of seconds, the lock clicked back and the door swung open.

The yarner squatted in its corner, a bright and lovely sight. Jiggered up, Jasper had affirmed. If someone else ever tried to use it, it would very likely burn out or kill him. But that had been just talk, just cover-up for his pig-headed selfishness.

Two weeks, Hart told himself. If he used his head he should be able to operate it without suspicion for at least two weeks. It would be easy. All he'd have to say was that Jasper had told him that he could borrow it any time he wished. And if he was any judge of character, Jasper would not be returning soon.

But even so, two weeks would be all the time he'd need. In two weeks, working day and night, he could turn out enough copy to buy himself a new machine.

He walked across the room to the yarner and pulled out the chair that stood in front of it. Calmly he sat down, reached out a hand and patted the instrument panel. It was a good machine. It turned out a lot of stuff—good stuff. Jasper had been selling steadily.

Good old yarner, Hart said.

He dropped his finger to the switch and flipped it over. Nothing happened. Startled, he flipped it back, flipped it on again. Still nothing happened.

He got up hastily to check the power connection. There was no power connection! For a shocked moment, he stood rooted to the floor.

Jiggered up, Jasper had said. Jiggered up so ingeniously that it could dispense with power?

It just wasn't possible. It was unthinkable. With fumbling fingers, he lifted the side panel, and peered inside.

The machine's innards were a mess. Half of the tubes were gone. Others were burned out, and the wiring had been ripped loose in places. The whole relay section was covered with dust. Some of the metal, he saw, was rusty. The entire machine was just a pile of junk.

He replaced the panel with suddenly shaking fingers, reeled back blindly and collided with a table. He clutched at it and held on tight to still the shaking of his hands, to steady the mad roaring in his head.

Jasper's machine wasn't jiggered up. It wasn't even in operating condition.

No wonder Jasper had kept his door locked. He lived in mortal fear that someone would find out that he wrote by hand!

And now despite the dirty trick he'd played on a worthy

116

friend, Hart was no better off than he had been before. He was faced with the same old problems, with no prospect of overcoming them. He still had his own beaten-up machine and nothing more. Maybe it would have been better if he had gone to Caph.

He walked to the door, paused there for an instant, and looked back. On the littered desk he could see Jasper's typewriter carefully half-buried by the litter, and giving the exact impression that it was never used.

Still, Jasper sold. Jasper sold almost every word he wrote. He sold—hunched over his desk with a pencil in his hand or hammering out the words on a muted typewriter. He sold without using the yarner at all, but keeping it all bright and polished, an empty, useless thing. He sold by using it as a shield against the banter and the disgust of all those others who talked so glibly and relied so much upon the metal and the magic of the ponderous contraption.

First it was told by mouth, Jasper had said that very evening. *Then it was writ by hand. Now it's fabricated by machine.*

And what's next, he'd asked—as if he had never doubted that there would be something next.

What next? thought Hart. Was this the end and all of Man—the moving gear, the clever glass and metal, the adroit electronics?

For the sake of Man's own dignity—his very sanity—there *had* to be a next. Mechanics, by their very nature, were a dead end. You could only get so clever. You could only go so far.

Jasper knew that. Jasper had found out. He had discarded the mechanistic aid and gone back to hand again.

Give a work of craftsmanship some economic value and Man would find a way to turn it out in quantity. Once furniture had been constructed lovingly by artisans who produced works of art that would last with pride through many generations. Then the machine had come and Man had turned out furniture that was purely functional, furniture that had little lasting value and no pride at all.

And writing had followed the same pattern. It had pride no longer. It had ceased to be an art, and become a commodity.

But what was a man to do? What *could* he do? Lock his door like Jasper and work through lonely hours with the bitter taste of nonconformity sharp within his mind, tormenting him night and day?

Hart walked out of the room with a look of torment in his eyes. He waited for a second to hear the lock click home. Then he went down the hall and slowly climbed the stairs.

The alien—the blanket and the face—was still lying on the bed. But now its eyes were open and it stared at him when he came and closed the door behind him.

He stopped just inside the door and the cold mediocrity of the room—all of its meanness and its poverty—rose up to clog his nostrils. He was hungry, sick at heart and lonely, and the yarner in the corner seemed to mock him.

Through the open window he could hear the rumble of a spaceship taking off across the river and the hooting of a tug as it warped a ship into a wharf.

He stumbled to the bed.

"Move over, you," he said to the wide-eyed alien, and tumbled down beside it. He turned his back to it and drew his knees up against his chest and lay huddled there.

He was right back where he'd started just the other morning. He still had no tape to do the job that Irving wanted. He still had a busted up haywire machine. He was without a camera and he wondered where he could borrow one—although there would be no sense of borrowing one if he didn't have the money to pay a character. He'd tried once to take film by stealth and he wouldn't try again. It wasn't worth the risk of going to prison for three or four years.

We love the wild and woollies, Green Shirt had said. *From there we get the going of far places.*

And while with Green Shirt it would be the bang-bangs and the wild and woollies, with some other race it would be a different type of fiction—race after race finding in this strange product of Earth a new world of enchantment. The far places of the mind, perhaps—or the far places of emotion. The basic differences were not too important.

Angela had said it was a lousy way to make a living. But she had only been letting off steam. All writers at times said approximately the same thing. In every age men and women of every known profession at some time must have said that theirs was a lousy way to make a living. At the moment they

118

might have meant it, but at other times they knew that it was not lousy because it was important.

And writing was important, too—tremendously important. Not so much because it meant the "going of far places," but because it sowed the seed of Earth—the seed of Earth's thinking and of Earth's logic—among the myriad stars.

They are out there waiting, Hart thought, for the stories that he would never write.

He would try, of course, despite all obstacles. He might even do as Jasper had done, scribbling madly with a sense of shame, feeling anachronistic and inadequate, dreading the day when someone would ferret out his secret, perhaps by deducing from a certain eccentricity of style that it was not machine-written.

For Jasper was wrong, of course. The trouble was not with the yarners nor with the principle of mechanistic writing. It was with Jasper himself—a deep psychopathic quirk that made a rebel of him. But even so he had remained a fearful and a hidden rebel who locked his door and kept his yarner polished, and carefully covered his typewriter with the litter on his desk so no one would suspect that he ever used it.

Hart felt warmer now and he seemed to be no longer hungry and suddenly he thought of one of those far places that Green Shirt had talked about. It was a grove of trees and a brook ran through the grove. There was a sense of peace and calm and a touch of majesty and foreverness about it. He heard birdsong and smelled the sharp, spice-like scent of water running in its mossy banks. He walked among the trees and the Gothic shape of them made the place seem like a church. As he walked he formed words within his mind—words put together so feelingly and so rightly and so carefully that no one who read them could mistake what he had to say. They would know not only the sight of the grove itself, but the sound and the smell of it and the foreverness that filled it to overflowing.

But even in his exaltation he sensed a threat within the Gothic shape and the feeling of foreverness. Some lurking intuition told him that the grove was a place to get away from. He tried for a moment to remember how he had gotten there, but there was no memory. It was as if he had become familiar with the grove only a second or two before and yet he knew that he had been walking beneath the sun-dappled foliage for what must have been hours or days.

He felt a tingling on his throat and raised a hand to brush it off and his hand touched something small and warm that brought him upright out of bed.

His hand tightened on the creature's neck. He was about to rip it from his chest when suddenly he recalled, full-blown, the odd circumstance he had tried to remember just the night before.

His grip relaxed and he let his hand drop to his side. He stood beside the bed, in the warm familiarity of the room, and felt the comfort of the blanket-creature upon his back and shoulders and around his throat.

He wasn't hungry and he wasn't tired and the sickness that he'd felt had somehow disappeared. He wasn't even worried and that was most unusual, for he was customarily worried.

Twelve hours before he had stood in the areaway with the blanket creature in his arms and had sought to pry out of a suddenly stubborn mind an explanation for the strange sense of recognition he'd experienced—the feeling that somewhere he had read or heard of the crying thing he'd found. Now, with it clasped around his back and clinging to his throat, he knew.

He strode across the room, with the blanket creature clinging to him, and took a book down from a narrow, six foot shelf. It was an old and tattered book, worn smooth by many hands, and it almost slipped from his clasp as he turned it over to read the title on the spine: *Fragments from Lost Writings*.

He reversed the volume and began to leaf through its pages. He knew now where to find what he was looking for. He remembered exactly where he had read about the thing upon his back.

He found the pages quickly enough—a few salvaged paragraphs from some story, written long ago and lost.

He skipped the first two pages, and came suddenly upon the paragraphs he wanted:

Ambitious vegetables, the life blankets waited, probably only obscurely aware of what they were waiting for. But when the humans came the long, long wait was over. The life blanket made a deal with men. And in the last analysis they turned out to be the greatest aid to galactic exploration that had ever been discovered.

And there it was, thought Hart—the old, smug pat assurance that it would be the humans who would go into the galaxy to explore it and make contact with its denizens and carry to every planet they visited the virtues of the Earth.

With a life blanket draped like a bobtailed cloak around his shoulders, a man had no need to worry about being fed, for the life blanket had the strange ability to gather energy and convert it into food for the body of its host.

It became, in fact, almost a second body—a watchful, fussy, quasiparental body that watched over the body of its host, keeping metabolism in balance despite alien conditions, rooting out infections, playing the role of mother, cook and family doctor combined.

But in return the blanket became, in a sense, the double of its host. Shedding its humdrum vegetable existence, it became vicariously a man, sharing all of its host's emotions and intelligence, living the kind of life it never could have lived if left to itself.

And not content with this fair trade the blankets threw in a bonus, a sort of dividend of gratitude. There were storytellers and imaginers. They could imagine anything—literally anything at all. They spent long hours spinning out tall yarns for the amusement of their hosts, serving as a shield against boredom and loneliness ...

There was more of it, but Hart did not need to read on. He turned back to the beginning of the fragment and he read: *Author Unknown. Circa 1956.*

Six hundred years ago! Six hundred years—and how could any man in 1956 have known?

The answer was he couldn't.

There was no way he could have known. He'd simply *dreamed* it up. And hit the truth dead center! Some early writer of science fiction had had an inspired vision!

There was something coming through the grove and it was a thing of utter beauty. It was not humanoid and it was not a monster. It was something no man had ever seen before. And yet despite the beauty of it, there was a deadly danger in it and something one must flee from.

He turned around to flee and found himself in the center of the room.

"All right," he said to the blanket. "Let's cut it out for now. We can go back later."

We can go back later and we can make a story of it and we can go many other places and make stories of them, too. I won't need a yarner to write those kind of stories, for I can recapture the excitement and splendor of it, and link it all together better than a yarner could. I'll have been there and lived it, and that's a setup you can't beat.

And there it was! The answer to the question that Jasper had asked, sitting at the table in the Bright Star bar.

What next?

And this was next: a symbiosis between Man and an alien thing, imagined centuries ago by a man whose very name was lost.

It was almost, Hart thought, as if God had placed His hand against his back and propelled him gently onward, for it was utterly fantastic that he should have found the answer crying in an areaway between an appartment house and a bindery.

But that did not matter now. The important thing was that he'd found it and brought it home—not quite knowing why at the time and wondering later why he had even bothered with it.

The important thing was that *now* was the big pay-off.

He heard footsteps coming up the stairs and turning down the hall. Alarmed by their rapid approach he reached up hastily and snatched the blanket from his shoulders. Frantically he looked about for a place to hide the creature. Of course! His desk. He jerked open the bottom drawer and stuffed the blanket into it, ignoring a slight resistance. He was kicking the drawer shut when Angela came into the room.

He could see at once that she was burned up.

"That was a lousy trick," she said. "You got Jasper into a lot of trouble."

Hart stared at her in consternation. "Trouble? You mean he didn't go to Caph."

"He's down in the basement hiding out. Blake told me he was there. I went down and talked to him."

"He got away from them?" Hart appeared badly shaken.

"Yes. He told them they didn't want a man at all. He told

122

them what they wanted was a machine and he told them about that glittering wonder—that Classic model—in the shop up-town."

"And so they went and stole it."

"No. If they had it would have been all right. But they bungled it. They smashed the glass to get at it, and that set off an alarm. Every cop in town came tearing after them."

"But Jasper was all—"

"They took Jasper with them to show them where it was."

Some of the color had returned to Hart's face. "And now Jasper's hiding from the law."

"That's the really bad part of it. He doesn't know whether he is or not. He's not sure the cops even saw him. What he's afraid of is that they might pick up one of those Caphians and sweat the story out of him. And if they do, Kemp Hart, you have a lot to answer for."

"Me? Why, I didn't do a thing—"

"Except tell them that Jasper was the man they wanted. How did you ever make them believe a line like that?"

"Easy. Remember what Jasper said. Everyone else tells the truth. We're the only ones who lie. Until they get wise to us, they'll believe every word we say. Because, you see, no one else tells anything but the truth and so—"

"Oh, shut up!" Angela said impatiently.

She looked around the room. "Where's that blanket thing?" she asked.

"It must have left. Maybe it ran away. When I came home it wasn't here."

"Haven't you any idea what it was?"

Hart shook his head. "Maybe it's just as well it's gone," he said. "It gave me a queasy feeling."

"You and Doc! That's another thing. This neighborhood's gone crazy. Doc is stretched out dead drunk under a tree in the park and there's an alien watching him. It won't let anyone come near him. It's as if it were guarding him, or had adopted him or something."

"Maybe it's one of Doc's pink elephants come to actual life. You know, dream a thing too often and—"

"It's no elephant and it isn't pink. It's got webbed feet that are too big for it and long, spindly legs. It's something like a spider, and its skin is warts. It has a triangular head with six

123

horns. It fairly makes you crawl just to look at it."

Hart shuddered. Ordinary aliens could be all right, but a thing like that—

"Wonder what it wants of Doc."

"Nobody seems to know. It won't talk."

"Maybe it can't talk."

"You know all aliens talk. At least enough of our language to make themselves understood. Otherwise they wouldn't come here."

"It sounds reasonable," said Hart. "Maybe it's acquiring a second-hand jag just sitting there beside Doc."

"Sometimes," said Angela, "your sense of humor is positively disgusting."

"Like writing books by hand."

"Yes," she said. "Like writing books by hand. You know as well as I do that people just don't talk about writing anything by hand. It's like—well, it's like eating with your fingers or belching in public or going without clothes."

"All right," he said, "all right. I'll never mention it again."

After she had left, Hart sat down and gave some serious thought to his situation.

In many ways he'd be a lot like Jasper, but he wouldn't mind if he could write as well as Jasper.

He'd have to start locking his door. He wondered where his key was. He never used it and now he'd have to look through his desk the first chance he got, to see if he couldn't locate it. If he couldn't find it, he'd have to have a new key made, because he couldn't have people walking in on him unexpectedly and catching him wearing the blanket or writing stuff by hand.

Maybe, he thought, it might be a good idea to move. It would be hard at times to explain why all at once he had started to lock his door. But he hated the thought of moving. Bad as it was, he'd gotten used to this place and it seemed like home.

Maybe, after he started selling, he should talk with Angela and see how she felt about moving in with him. Angela was a good kid, but you couldn't ask a girl to move in with you when you were always wondering where the next meal was coming from. But now, even if he didn't sell, he'd never have to worry where his next meal was coming from. He wondered briefly if the blanket could be shared as a food provider by two persons and he wondered how in the world he'd ever manage to explain it all to Angela.

And how had that fellow back in 1956 ever thought of such a thing? How many of the other wild ideas concocted out of tortuous mental efforts and empty whiskey bottles might be true as well?

A dream? An idea? A glimmer of the future? It did not matter which, for a man had thought of it and it had come true. How many of the other things that Man had thought of in the past and would think of in the future would also become the truth?

The idea scared him.

That "going of far places". The reaching out of the imagination. The influence of the written word, the thought and power behind it. It was deadlier than a battleship, he'd said. How everlastingly right he had been.

He got up and walked across the room and stood in front of the yarner. It leered at him. He stuck out his tongue at it.

"That for you," he said.

Behind him he heard a rustle and hastily whirled about.

The blanket had somehow managed to ooze out of the desk drawer and it was heading for the door, reared upon the nether folds of its flimsy body. It was slithering along in a jerky fashion like a wounded seal.

"Hey, you!" yelled Hart and made a grab at it. But he was too late. A being—there was no other word for it—stood in the doorway and the blanket reached it and slithered swiftly up its body and plastered itself upon its back.

The thing in the doorway hissed at Hart: "I lose it. You are so kind to keep it. I am very grateful."

Hart stood transfixed.

The creature was a sight. Just like the one which Angela had seen guarding Doc, only possibly a little uglier. It had webbed feet that were three times too big for it, so that it seemed to be wearing snowshoes, and it had a tail that curved ungracefully halfway up its back. It had a melon-shaped head with a triangular face, and six horns and there were rotating eyes on top of each and every horn.

The monstrosity dipped into a pouch that seemed to be part of its body, and took out a roll of bills.

"So small a reward," it piped and tossed the bills to Hart.

Hart put out a hand and caught them absentmindedly.

"We go now," said the being. "We think kind thoughts of you."

It had started to turn around, but at Hart's bellow of protest it swiveled back.

"Yes, good sir?"

"This—blanket—this thing I found. What about it?"

"We make it."

"But it's alive and—"

The thing grinned a murderous grin. "You so clever people. You think it up. Many times ago."

"That story!"

"Quite so. We read of it. We make it. Very good idea."

"You can't mean you actually—"

"We biologist. What you call them—biologic engineers."

It turned about and started down the hall.

Hart howled after it. "Just a minute! Hold up there! Just a min—"

But it was going fast and it didn't stop. Hart thundered after it. When he reached the head of the stairs and glanced down it was out of sight. But he raced after it, taking the stairs three at a time in defiance of all the laws of safety.

He didn't catch it. In the street outside he pulled to a halt and looked in all directions but there was no sign of it. It had completely disappeared.

He reached into his pocket and felt the roll of bills he had caught on the fly. He pulled the roll out and it was bigger than he remembered it. He snapped off the rubber band, and examined a few of the bills separately. The denomination on the top bill, in galactic credits, was so big it staggered him. He riffled through the entire sheaf of bills and all the denominations seemed to be the same.

He gasped at the thought of it, and rifled through them once again. He had been right the first time—all the denominations *were* the same. He did a bit of rapid calculation and it was strictly unbelievable. In credits, too—and a credit was convertible, roughly into five Earth dollars.

He had seen credits before, but never actually held one in his hand. They were the currency of galactic trade and were widely used in interstellar banking circles, but seldom drifted down into general circulation. He held them in his hand and took a good look at them and they sure were beautiful.

The being must have immeasurably prized that blanket, he thought—to give him such a fabulous sum simply for taking care of it. Although, when you came to think of it, it wasn't necessarily so. Standards of wealth differed greatly from one planet to another and the fortune he held in his hands might have been little more than pocket money to the blanket's owner.

He was surprised to find that he wasn't too thrilled or happy, as he should have been. All he seemed to be able to think about was that he'd lost the blanket.

He thrust the bills into his pocket and walked across the street to the little park. Doc was awake and sitting on a bench underneath a tree. Hart sat down beside him.

"How you feeling, Doc?" he asked.

"I'm feeling all right, son," the old man replied.

"Did you see an alien, like a spider wearing snow-shoes?"

"There was one of them here just a while ago. It was here when I woke up. It wanted to know about that thing you'd found."

"And you told it."

"Sure. Why not? It said it was hunting for it. I figured you'd be glad to get it off your hands."

The two of them sat silently for a while.

Then Hart asked, "Doc, what would you do if you had about a billion bucks?"

"Me," said Doc, without the slightest hesitation, "I'd drink myself to death. Yes, sir, I'd drink myself to death real fancy, not on any of this rotgut they sell in this end of town."

And that was the way it went, thought Hart. Doc would drink himself to death. Angela would go in for arty salons and the latest styles. Jasper more than likely would buy a place out in the mountains where he could be away from people.

And me, thought Hart, what will I do with a billion bucks give or take a million?

Yesterday, last night, up until a couple of hours ago, he would have traded in his soul on the Classic yarner.

But now it seemed all sour and offbeat.

For there was a better way—the way of symbiosis, the teaming up of Man and an alien biologic concept.

He remembered the grove with its Gothic trees and its sense

127

of foreverness and even yet, in the brightness of the sun, he shivered at the thought of the thing of beauty that had appeared among the trees.

That was, he told himself, a surely better way to write—to know the thing yourself and write it, to live the yarn and write it.

But he had lost the blanket and he didn't know where to find another. He didn't even know, if he found the place they came from, what he'd have to do to capture it.

An alien biologic concept, and yet not entirely alien, for it had first been thought of by an unknown man six centuries before. A man who had written as Jasper wrote even in this day, hunched above a table, scribbling out the words he put together in his brain. No yarner there—no tapes, no films, none of the other gadgets. But even so that unknown man had reached across the mists of time and space to touch another unknown mind and the life blanket had come alive as surely as if Man himself had made it.

And was that the true greatness of the human race—that they could imagine something and in time it would be so?

And if that were the greatness, could Man afford to delegate it to the turning shaft, the spinning wheel, the clever tubes, the innards of machines?

"You wouldn't happen," asked Doc, "to have a dollar on you?"

"No," said Hart, "I haven't got a dollar."

"You're just like the rest of us," said Doc. "You dream about the billions and you haven't got a dime."

Jasper was a rebel and it wasn't worth it. All the rebels ever got were the bloody noses and the broken heads.

"I could sure use a buck," said Doc.

It wasn't worth it to Jasper Hansen and it wasn't worth it to the others who must also lock their doors and polish up their never-used machines, so that when someone happened to drop in they'd see them standing there.

And it isn't worth it to me, Kemp Hart told himself. Not when by continuing to conform he could become famous almost automatically and virtually overnight.

He put his hand into his pocket and felt the roll of bills and knew that in just a little while he'd go uptown and buy that wonderful machine. There was plenty in the roll to buy it.

With what there was in that roll he could buy a shipload of them.

"Yes, sir," said Doc harking back to his answer to the billion dollar question. "It would be a pleasant death. A pleasant death, indeed."

A gang of workmen were replacing the broken window when Hart arrived at the uptown showroom, but he scarcely more than glanced at them and walked straight inside.

The same salesman seemed to materialize from thin air.

But he wasn't happy. His expression was stern and a little pained.

"You've come back, no doubt," he said, "to place an order for the Classic."

"That is right," said Hart and pulled the roll out of his pocket.

The salesman was well-trained. He stood walleyed for just a second, then recovered his composure with a speed which must have set a record.

"That's fine," he said. "I knew you'd be back. I was telling some of the other men this morning that you would be coming in."

I just bet you were, thought Hart.

"I suppose," he said, that if I paid you cash you would consider throwing in a rather generous supply of tapes and films and some of the other stuff I need."

"Certainly, sir. I'll do the best I can for you."

Hart peeled off twenty-five thousand and put the rest back in his pocket.

"Won't you have a seat," the salesman urged. "I'll be right back. I'll arrange delivery and fix up the guarantee..."

"Take your time," Hart told him, enjoying every minute of it.

He sat down in a chair and did a little planning.

First he'd have to move to better quarters and as soon as he had moved he'd have a dinner for the crowd and he'd rub Jasper's nose in it. He'd certainly do it—if Jasper wasn't tucked away in jail. He chuckled to himself, thinking of Jasper cringing in the basement of the Bright Star bar.

And this very afternoon he'd go over to Irving's office and pay him back the twenty and explain how it was he couldn't

129

find the time to write the stuff he wanted.

Not that he wouldn't have liked to help Irving out. But it would be sacrilege to write the kind of junk that Irving wanted on a machine as talented as the Classic.

He heard footsteps coming hurriedly across the floor behind him and he stood up and turned around, smiling at the salesman.

But the salesman wasn't smiling. He was close to apoplexy.

"You!" said the salesman, choking just a little in his attempt to remain a gentleman. "That money! We've had enough from you, young man."

"The money," said Hart. "Why, it's galactic credits. It—"

"It's play money," stormed the salesman. "Money for the kids. Play money from the Draconian federation. It says so, right on the face of it. In those big characters."

He handed Hart the money.

"Get out of here!" the salesman shouted.

"But," Hart pleaded, "are you sure? It can't be! You must be mistaken—"

"Our teller says it is. He has to be an expert on all sorts of money and *he says it is*!"

"But you took it. You couldn't tell the difference."

"I can't read Draconian. But the teller can."

"That damn alien!" shouted Hart in sudden fury. "Just let me get my hands on him!"

The salesman softened just a little.

"You can't trust those aliens, sir. They are a sneaky lot."

"Get out of my way," Hart shouted. "I've got to find that alien!"

The man at the Alien bureau wasn't very helpful.

"We have no record," he told Hart, "of the kind of creature you describe. You wouldn't have a photo of it, would you?"

"No," said Hart. "I haven't got a photo."

The man started piling up the catalogs he had been looking through.

"Of course," he said, "the fact we have no record of him doesn't mean a thing. Admittedly, we can't keep track of all the various people. There are so many of them and new ones all the time. Perhaps you might inquire at the spaceport. Someone might have seen your alien."

"I've already done that. Nothing. Nothing at all. He must have come in and possibly have gone back, but no one can remember him. Or maybe they won't tell."

"The aliens hang together," said the man. "They don't tell you nothing."

He went on stacking up the books. It was near to quitting time and he was anxious to be off.

The man said, jokingly, "You might go out in space and try to hunt him up."

"I might do just that," said Hart and left, slamming the door behind him.

Joke: You might go out in space and find him. You might go out and track him across ten thousand light-years and among a million stars. And when you found him you might say I want to have a blanket and he'd laugh right in your face.

But by the time you'd tracked him across ten thousand light-years and among a million stars you'd no longer need a blanket, for you would have lived your stories and you would have seen your characters and you would have absorbed ten thousand backgrounds and a million atmospheres.

And you'd need no yarner and no tapes and films, for the words would be pulsing at your fingertips and pounding in your brain, shrieking to get out.

Joke: Toss a backwoods yokel a fistful of play money for something worth a million. The fool wouldn't know the difference until he tried to spend it. Be a big shot cheap and then go off in a corner by yourself and die laughing at how superior you are.

And who had it been that said humans were the only liars?

Joke: Wear a blanket around your shoulders and send your ships to Earth for the drivel that they write there—never knowing, never guessing that you have upon your back the very thing that's needed to break Earth's monopoly on fiction.

And that, said Hart, *is a joke on you.*

If I ever find you, I'll cram it down your throat.

Angela came up the stairs bearing an offering of peace. She set the kettle on the table. "Some soup," she said. "I'm good at making soup."

"Thanks, Angela," he said. "I forgot to eat today."

"Why the knapsack, Kemp? Going on a hike?"

"No, going on vacation."

"But you didn't tell me."

"I just now made up my mind to go. A little while ago."

"I'm sorry I was so angry at you. It turned out all right. Green Shirt and his gang made their getaway."

"So Jasper can come out."

"He's already out. He's plenty sore at you."

"That's all right with me. I'm no pal of his."

She sat down in a chair and watched him pack.

"Where are you going, Kemp?"

"I'm hunting for an alien."

"Here in the city? Kemp, you'll never find him."

"Not in the city. I'll have to ask around."

"But there aren't any aliens—"

"That's right."

"You're a crazy fool," she cried. "You can't do it, Kemp. I won't let you. How will you live? What will you do?"

"I'll write."

"Write? You can't write! Not without a yarner."

"I'll write by hand. Indecent as it may be, I'll write by hand because I'll know the things I write about. It'll be in my blood and at my fingertips. I'll have the smell of it and the color of it and the taste of it!"

She leaped from the chair and beat at his chest with tiny fits.

"It's filthy! It's uncivilized! It's—"

"That's the way they wrote before. All the millions of stories, all the great ideas, all the phrases that you love to quote. And that is the way it should have stayed. This is a dead-end street we're on."

"You'll come back," she said. "You'll find that you are wrong and you'll come back."

He shook his head at her. "Not until I find my alien."

"It isn't any alien you are after. It is something else. I can see it in you."

She whirled around and raced out the door and down the stairs.

He went back to his packing and when he had finished, he sat down and ate the soup. Angela, he thought, was right. She was good at making soup.

And she was right in another thing as well. It was no alien he was seeking.

For he didn't need an alien. And he didn't need a blanket and he didn't need a yarner.

He took the kettle to the sink and washed it beneath the tap and dried it carefully. Then he set it in the center of the table where Angela, when she came, would be sure to see it.

Then he took up the knapsack and started slowly down the stairs.

He had reached the street when he heard the cry behind him. It was Angela and she was running after him. He stopped and waited for her.

"I'm going with you, Kemp."

"You don't know what you're saying. It'll be rough and hard. Strange lands and alien people. And we haven't any money."

"Yes, we have. We have that fifty. The one I tried to loan you. It's all I have and it won't go far, I know. But we have it."

"You're looking for no alien."

"Yes, I am. I'm looking for an alien, too. All of us, I think, are looking for your alien."

He reached out an arm and swept her roughly to him, held her close against him.

"Thank you, Angela," he said.

Hand in hand they headed for the spaceport, looking for a ship that would take them to the stars.

GALACTIC CHEST

I had just finished writing the daily Community Chest story, and each day I wrote that story I was sore about it; there were plenty of punks in the office who could have ground out that kind of copy. Even the copy boys could have written it and no one would have known the difference; no one ever read it—except maybe some of the drive chairmen, and I'm not even sure about them reading it.

I had protested to Barnacle Bill about my handling the Community Chest for another year. I had protested loud. I had said: "Now, you know, Barnacle, I been writing that thing for three or four years. I write it with my eyes shut. You ought to get some new blood into it. Give one of the cubs a chance; they can breathe some life into it. Me, I'm all written out on it."

But it didn't do a bit of good. The Barnacle had me down on the assignment book for the Community Chest, and he never changed a thing once he put it in the book.

I wish I knew the real reason for that name of his. I've heard a lot of stories about how it was hung on him, but I don't think there's any truth in them. I think he got it simply from the way he can hang on to a bar.

I had just finished writing the Community Chest story and was sitting there, killing time and hating myself, when along came Jo Ann. Jo Ann was the sob sister on the paper; she got some lousy yarns to write, and that's a somber fact. I guess it was because I am of a sympathetic nature, and took pity on her, and let her cry upon my shoulder that we got to know each other so well. By now, of course, we figure we're in love; off and on we talk about getting married, as soon as I snag that foreign correspondent job I've been angling for.

"Hi, kid," I said.

And she says, "Do you know, Mark, what the Barnacle has me down for today?"

"He's finally ferreted out a one-armed paperhanger," I guessed, "and he wants you to do a feature. . . ."

"It's worse than that," she moans. "It's an old lady who is celebrating her one hundredth birthday."

"Maybe," I said, "she will give you a piece of her birthday cake."

"I don't see how even you can joke about a thing like this," Jo Ann told me. "It's positively ghastly."

Just then the Barnacle let out a bellow for me. So I picked up the Community Chest story and went over to the city desk.

Barnacle Bill is up to his elbows in copy; the phone is ringing and he's ignoring it, and for this early in the morning he has worked himself into more than a customary lather. "You remember old Mrs. Clayborne?"

"Sure, she's dead. I wrote the obit on her ten days or so ago."

"Well, I want you to go over to the house and snoop around a bit."

"What for?" I asked. "She hasn't come back, has she?"

"No, but there's some funny business over there. I got a tip that someone might have hurried her a little."

"This time," I told him, "you've outdone yourself. You've been watching too many television thrillers."

"I got it on good authority," he said and turned back to his work.

So I went and got my hat and told myself it was no skin off my nose how I spent the day; I'd get paid just the same!

But I was getting a little fed up with some of the wild-goose chases to which the Barnacle was assigning not only me, but the rest of the staff as well. Sometimes they paid off; usually, they didn't. And when they didn't, Barnacle had the nasty habit of making it appear that the man he had sent out, not he himself, had dreamed up the chase. His "good authority" probably was no more than some casual chatter of someone next to him at the latest bar he'd honored with his cash.

Old Mrs. Clayborne had been one of the last of the faded gentility which at one time had graced Douglas Avenue. The family had petered out, and she was the last of them; she had died in a big and lonely house with only a few servants, and a nurse in attendance on her, and no kin close enough to wait out her final hours in person.

It was unlikely, I told myself, that anyone could have profited by giving her an overdose of drugs, or otherwise hurrying her death. And even if it was true, there'd be little chance that it could be proved; and that was the kind of story you didn't run unless you had it down in black and white.

I went to the house on Douglas Avenue. It was a quiet and lovely place, standing in its fenced-in yard among the autumn-colored trees.

There was an old gardener raking leaves, and he didn't notice me when I went up the walk. He was an old man, pottering away and more than likely mumbling to himself, and I found out later that he was a little deaf.

I went up the steps, rang the bell and stood waiting, feeling cold at heart and wondering what I'd say once I got inside. I couldn't say what I had in mind; somehow or other I'd have to go about it by devious indirection.

A maid came to the door.

"Good morning, ma'am," I said. "I am from the *Tribune*. May I come in and talk?"

She didn't even answer; she looked at me for a moment and then slammed the door. I told myself I might have known that was the way it would be.

I turned around, went down the steps, and cut across the grounds to where the gardener was working. He didn't notice me until I was almost upon him; when he did see me, his face sort of lit up. He dropped the rake, and sat down on the wheelbarrow. I suppose I was as good an excuse as any for him to take a breather.

"Hello," I said to him.

"Nice day," he said to me.

"Indeed it is."

"You'll have to speak up louder," he told me; "I can't hear a thing you say."

"Too bad about Mrs. Clayborne," I told him.

"Yes, yes," he said. "You live around here? I don't recall your face."

I nodded; it wasn't much of a lie, just twenty miles or so.

"She was a nice old lady. Worked for her almost fifty years. It's a blessing she is gone."

"I suppose it is."

"She was dying hard," he said.

He sat nodding in the autumn sun and you could almost hear his mind go traveling back across those fifty years. I am certain that, momentarily, he'd forgotten I was there.

"Nurse tells a funny story," he said finally, speaking to himself more than he spoke to me. "It might be just imagining; Nurse was tired, you know."

"I heard about it," I encouraged him.

"Nurse left her just a minute and she swears there was something in the room when she came back again. Says it went out the window, just as she came in. Too dark to see it good,

136

she says. I told her she was imagining. Funny things happen, though; things we don't know about."

"That was her room," I said, pointing at the house. "I remember, years ago . . ."

He chuckled at having caught me in the wrong. "You're mistaken, sonny. It was the corner one; that one over there."

He rose from the barrow slowly and took up the rake again.

"It was good to talk with you," I said. "These are pretty flowers you have. Mind if I walk around and have a look at them?"

"Might as well. Frost will get them in a week or so."

So I walked around the grounds, hating myself for what I had to do, and looking at the flowers, working my way closer to the corner of the house he had pointed out to me.

There was a bed of petunias underneath the window and they were sorry-looking things. I squatted down and pretended I was admiring them, although all the time I was looking for some evidence that someone might have jumped out the window.

I didn't expect to find it, but I did.

There, in a little piece of soft earth where the petunias had petered out, was a footprint—well, not a footprint, either, maybe, but anyhow a print. It looked something like a duck track—except that the duck that made it would have had to be as big as a good-sized dog.

I squatted on the walk, staring at it and I could feel spiders on my spine. Finally I got up and walked away, forcing myself to saunter when my body screamed to run.

Outside the gate I *did* run.

I got to a phone as fast as I could, at a corner drugstore, and sat in the booth a while to get my breathing back to normal before I put in a call to the city desk.

The Barnacle bellowed at me. "What you got?"

"I don't know," I said. "Maybe nothing. Who was Mrs. Clayborne's doctor?"

He told me. I asked him if he knew who her nurse had been, and he asked how the hell should he know, so I hung up.

I went to see the doctor and he threw me out.

I spent the rest of the day tracking down the nurse; when I finally found her she threw me out too. So there was a full day's work gone entirely down the drain.

It was late in the afternoon when I got back to the office. Barnacle Bill pounced on me at once. "What did you get?"

"Nothing," I told him. There was no use telling him about that track underneath the window. By that time, I was beginning to doubt I'd ever seen it, it seemed so unbelievable.

"How big do ducks get?" I asked him. He growled at me and went back to his work.

I looked at the next day's page in the assignment book. He had me down for the Community Chest, and: *See Dr. Thomas at Univ.—magnetism.*

"What's this?" I asked. "This magnetism business?"

"Guy's been working on it for years," said the Barnacle. "I got it on good authority he's set to pop with something."

There was that "good authority" again. And just about as hazy as the most of his hot tips.

And anyhow, I don't like to interview scientists. More often than not, they're a crochety set and are apt to look down their noses at newspapermen. Ten to one the newspaperman is earning more than they are—and in his own way more than likely, doing just as good a job and with less fumbling.

I saw that Jo Ann was getting ready to go home, so I walked over to her and asked her how it went.

"I got a funny feeling in my gizzard, Mark," she told me. "Buy me a drink and I'll tell you all about it."

So we went down to the corner and took a booth way in the back.

Joe came over and he was grumbling about business, which was unusual for him. "If it weren't for you folks over at the paper," he said, "I'd close up and go home. That must be what all my customers are doing; they sure ain't coming here. Can you think of anything more disgusting than going straight home from your job?"

We told him that we couldn't, and to show that he appreciated our attitude he wiped off the table—a thing he almost never did.

He brought the drinks and Jo Ann told me about the old lady and her hundredth birthday. "It was horrible. There she sat in her rocking chair in that bare living room, rocking back and forth, gently, delicately, the way old ladies rock. And she was glad to see me, and she smiled so nice and she introduced me all around."

"Well that was fine," I said. "Were there a lot of people there?"

"Not a soul."

I choked on my drink. "But you said she introduced..."

"She did. To empty chairs."

"Good Lord!"

"They all were dead," she said.

"Now, let's get this straight..."

"She said, 'Miss Evans, I want you to meet my old friend, Mrs. Smith. She lives just down the street. I recall the day she moved into the neighborhood, back in '33. Those were hard times, I tell you." Chattering on, you know, like most old ladies do. And me, standing there and staring at an empty chair, wondering what to do. And, Mark, I don't know if I did right or not, but I said, 'Hello, Mrs. Smith. I am glad to know you.' And do you know what happened then?"

"No," I said. "How could I?"

"The old lady said, just as casually as could be—just conversationally, as if it were the most natural thing in all the world—'You know, Miss Evans, Mrs. Smith died three years ago. Don't you think it's nice she dropped in to see me?' "

"She was pulling your leg," I said. "Some of these old ones sometimes get pretty sly."

"I don't think she was. She introduced me all around; there were six or seven of them, and all of them were dead."

"She was happy, thinking they were there. What difference does it make?"

"It was horrible," said Jo Ann.

So we had another drink to chase away the horror.

Joe was still down in the mouth. "Did you ever see the like of it? You could shoot off a cannon in this joint and not touch a single soul. By this time, usually, they'd be lined up against the bar, and it'd be a dull evening if someone hadn't taken a poke at someone else—although you understand I run a decent place."

"Sure you do," I said. "Sit down and have a drink with us."

"It ain't right that I should," said Joe. "A bartender should never take a drink when he's conducting business. But I feel so

139

low that if you don't mind, I'll take you up on it."

He went back to the bar and got a bottle and a glass and we had quite a few.

The corner, he said, had always been a good spot—steady business all the time, with a rush at noon and a good crowd in the evening. But business had started dropping off six weeks before, and now was down to nothing.

"It's the same all over town," he said, "some places worse than others. This place is one of the worst; I just don't know what's gotten into people."

We said we didn't, either. I fished out some money and left it for the drinks, and we made our escape.

Outside I asked Jo Ann to have dinner with me, but she said it was the night her bridge club met, so I drove her home and went on to my place.

I take a lot of ribbing at the office for living so far out of town, but I like it. I got the cottage cheap, and it's better than living in a couple of cooped-up rooms in a third-rate resident hotel—which would be the best I could afford if I stayed in town.

After I'd fixed up a steak and some fried potatoes for supper, I went down to the dock and rowed out into the lake a ways. I sat there for a while, watching the lighted windows winking all around the shore and listening to the sounds you never hear in daytime—the muskrat swimming and the soft chuckling of the ducks and the occasional slap of a jumping fish.

It was a bit chilly and after a little while I rowed back in again, thinking there was a lot to do before winter came. The boat should be caulked and painted; the cottage itself could take a coat of paint, if I could get around to it. There were a couple of storm windows that needed glass replaced, and by rights I should putty all of them. The chimney needed some bricks to replace the ones that had blown off in a windstorm earlier in the year, and the door should have new weather-stripping.

I sat around and read a while and then I went to bed. Just before I went to sleep I thought some about the two old ladies—one of them happy and the other dead.

The next morning I got the Community Chest story out of the way, first thing; then I got an encyclopedia from the library

140

and did some reading on magnetism. I figured that I should know something about it, before I saw this whiz-bang at the university.

But I needn't have worried so much; this Dr. Thomas turned out to be a regular Joe. We sat around and had quite a talk. He told me about magnetism, and when he found out I lived at the lake he talked about fishing; then we found we knew some of the same people, and it was all right.

Except he didn't have a story.

"There may be one in another year or so," he told me. "When there is, I'll let you in on it."

I'd heard that one before, of course, so I tried to pin him down.

"It's a promise," he said; "you get it first, ahead of anyone."

I let it go at that. You couldn't ask the man to sign a contract on it.

I was watching for a chance to get away, but I could see he still had more to say. So I stayed on; it's refreshing to find someone who wants to talk to you.

"I think there'll be a story," he said, looking worried, as if he were afraid there mightn't be. "I've worked on it for years. Magnetism is still one of the phenomena we don't know too much about. Once we knew nothing about electricity, and even now we do not entirely understand it; but we found out about it, and when we knew enough about it, we put it to work. We could do the same with magnetism, perhaps—if we only could determine the first fundamentals of it."

He stopped and looked straight at me. "When you were a kid, did you believe in brownies?"

That one threw me and he must have seen it did.

"You remember—the little helpful people. If they liked you, they did all sorts of things for you; and all they expected of you was that you'd leave out a bowl of milk for them."

I told him I'd read the stories, and I supposed that at one time I must have believed in them—although right at the moment I couldn't swear I had.

"If I didn't know better," he said, "I'd think I had brownies in this lab. Someone—or something—shuffled my notes for me. I'd left them on the desktop held down with a paperweight; the next morning they were spread all over, and part of them dumped onto the floor."

141

"A cleaning woman," I suggested.

He smiled at my suggestion. "I'm the cleaning woman here."

I thought he had finished and I wondered why all this talk of notes and brownies. I was reaching for my hat when he told me the rest of it.

"There were two sheets of the notes still underneath the paperweight," he said. "One of them had been folded carefully. I was about to pick them up, and put them with the other sheets so I could sort them later, when I happened to read what was on those sheets beneath the paperweight."

He drew a long breath. "They were two sections of my notes that, if left to myself, I probably never would have tied together. Sometimes we have strange blind spots; sometimes we look so closely at a thing that we are blinded to it. And there it was—two sheets laid there by accident. Two sheets, one of them folded to tie up with the other, to show me a possibility I'd never have thought of otherwise. I've been working on that possibility ever since; I have hopes it may work out."

"When it does . . ." I said.

"It is yours," he told me.

I got my hat and left.

And I thought idly of brownies all the way back to the office.

I had just got back to the office, and settled down for an hour or two of loafing, when old J. H.—our publisher—made one of his irregular pilgrimages of good will out into the newsroom. J. H. is a pompous windbag, without a sincere bone in his body; he knows we know this and we know he knows—but he, and all the rest of us, carry out the comedy of good fellowship to its bitter end.

He stopped beside my desk, clapped me on the shoulder, and said in a voice that boomed throughout the newsroom: "That's a tremendous job you're doing on the Community Chest, my boy."

Feeling a little sick and silly, I got to my feet and said, "Thank you, J. H.; it's nice of you to say so."

Which was what was expected of me. It was almost ritual.

He grabbed me by the hand, put the other hand on my shoulder, shook my hand vigorously and squeezed my shoulder hard. And I'll be damned if there weren't tears in his eyes as he told me, "You just stick around, Mark, and keep up the good work. You won't regret it for a minute. We may not always show it, but we appreciate good work and loyalty and we're always watching what you do out here."

Then he dropped me like a hot potato and went on with his greetings.

I sat down again; the rest of the day was ruined for me. I told myself that if I deserved any commendation I could have hoped it would be for something other than the Community Chest stories. They were lousy stories; I knew it, and so did the Barnacle and all the rest of them. No one blamed me for their being lousy—you can't write anything but a lousy story on a Community Chest drive. But they weren't cheering me.

And I had a sinking feeling that, somehow, old J. H. had found out about the applications I had planted with a half dozen other papers and that this was his gentle way of letting me know he knew—and that I had better watch my step.

Just before noon, Steve Johnson—who handles the medical run along with whatever else the Barnacle can find for him to do—came over to my desk. He had a bunch of clippings in his hand and he was looking worried. "I hate to ask you this, Mark," he said, "but would you help me out?"

"Sure thing, Steve."

"It's an operation. I have to check on it, but I won't have the time. I got to run out to the airport and catch an interview."

He laid the clips down on my desk. "It's all in there."

Then he was off for his interview.

I picked up the clippings and read them through; it was a story that would break your heart.

There was this little fellow, about three years old, who had to have an operation on his heart. It was a piece of surgery that had been done only a time or two before, and then only in big Eastern hospitals by famous medical names—and never on one as young as three.

I hated to pick up the phone and call; I was almost sure the kind of answer I would get.

But I did, and naturally I ran into the kind of trouble you always run into when you try to get some information out of a hospital staff—as if they were shining pure and you were a dirty little mongrel trying to sneak in. But I finally got hold of

143

someone who told me the boy seemed to be okay and that the operation appeared to be successful.

So I called the surgeon who had done the job. I must have caught him in one of his better moments, for he filled me in on some information that fit into the story.

"You are to be congratulated, Doctor," I told him and he got a little testy.

"Young man," he told me, "in an operation such as this the surgeon is no more than a single factor. There are so many other factors that no one can take credit."

Then suddenly he sounded tired and scared. "It was a miracle," he said.

"But don't you quote me on that," he fairly shouted at me.

"I wouldn't think of it," I told him.

Then I called the hospital again, and talked to the mother of the boy.

It was a good story. We caught the home edition with it, a four-column head on the left side of page one, and the Barnacle gave me a byline on it.

After lunch I went back to Jo Ann's desk; she was in a tizzy. The Barnacle had thrown a church convention program at her and she was in the midst of writing an advance story, listing all the speakers and committee members and special panels and events. It's the deadliest kind of a story you can be told to write; it's worse, even, than the Community Chest.

I listened to her being bitter for quite a while; then I asked her if she figured she'd have any strength left when the day was over.

"I'm all pooped out," she said.

"Reason I asked," I told her, "is that I want to take the boat out of the water and I need someone to help me."

"Mark," she said, "if you expect me to go out there and horse a boat around ..."

"You wouldn't have to lift," I told her. "Maybe just tug a little. We'll use a block and tackle to lift it on the blocks so that I can paint it later. All I need is someone to steady it while I haul it up."

She still wasn't sold on it, so I laid out some bait.

"We could stop downtown and pick up a couple of lobsters," I told her. "You are good at lobsters. I could make some of my Roquefort dressing, and we could have a ..."

144

"But without the garlic," she said. So I promised to forego the garlic and she agreed to come.

Somehow or other, we never did get that boat out of the water; there were so many other things to do.

After dinner we built a fire in the fireplace and sat in front of it. She put her head on my shoulder and we were comfortable and cozy. "Let's play pretend," she said. "Let's pretend you have that job you want. Let's say it is in London, and this is a lodge in the English fens...."

"A fen," I said, "is a hell of a place to have a lodge."

"You always spoil things," she complained. "Let's start over again. Let's pretend you have that job you want..."

And she stuck to her fens.

Driving back to the lake after taking her home, I wondered if I'd ever get that job. Right at the moment it didn't look so rosy. Not that I couldn't have handled it, for I knew I could. I had racks of books on world affairs, and I kept close track of what was going on. I had a good command of French, a working knowledge of German, and off and on I was struggling with Spanish. It was something I'd wanted all my life—to feel that I was part of that fabulous newspaper fraternity which kept check around the world.

I overslept, and was late to work in the morning. The Barnacle took a sour view of it. "Why did you bother to come in at all?" he growled at me. "Why do you ever bother to come in? Last two days I sent you out on two assignments, and where are the stories?"

"There weren't any stories," I told him, trying to keep my temper. "They were just some more pipe dreams you dug up."

"Some day," he said, "when you get to be a real reporter, you'll dig up stories for yourself. That's what's the matter with this staff," he said in a sudden burst of anger. "That's what's wrong with you. No initiative; sit around and wait; wait until I dig up something I can send you out on. No one ever surprises me and brings in a story I haven't sent them out on."

He pegged me with his eyes. "Why don't you just once surprise me?"

"I'll surprise you, buster," I said and walked over to my desk.

I sat there thinking. I thought about old Mrs. Clayborne, who had been dying hard—and then suddenly had died easy. I remembered what the gardener had told me, and the footprint I had found underneath the window. I thought of that other old lady who had been a hundred years old, and how all her old, dead friends had come visiting. And about the physicist who had brownies in his lab. And about the boy and his successful operation.

And I got an idea.

I went to the files and went through them three weeks back, page by page. I took a lot of notes and got a little scared, but told myself it was nothing but coincidence.

Then I sat down at my typewriter and made half a dozen false starts, but finally I had it.

The brownies have come back again, I wrote.

You know, those little people who do all sorts of good deeds for you, and expect nothing in return except that you set out a bowl of milk for them.

At the time I didn't realize that I was using almost the exact words the physicist had said.

I didn't write about Mrs. Clayborne, or the old lady with her visitors, or the physicist, or the little boy who had the operation; those weren't things you could write about with your tongue in cheek, and that's the way I wrote it.

But I did write about the little two and three paragraph items I had found tucked away in the issues I had gone through—the good luck stories; the little happy stories of no consequence, except for the ones they had happened to—about people finding things they'd lost months or years ago, about stray dogs coming home, and kids winning essay contests, and neighbor helping neighbor. All the kindly little news stories that we'd thrown in just to fill up awkward holes.

There were a lot of them—a lot more, it seemed to me, than you could normally expect to find. *All these things happened in our town in the last three weeks*, I wrote at the end of it.

And I added one last line: *Have you put out that bowl of milk?*

After it was finished, I sat there for a while, debating whether I should hand it in. And thinking it over, I decided that the Barnacle had it coming to him, after the way he'd shot off his mouth.

So I threw it into the basket on the city desk and went back to write the Community Chest story.

The Barnacle never said a thing to me and I didn't say a thing to him; you could have knocked my eyes off with a stick when the kid brought the papers up from the pressroom, and there was my brownie story spread across the top of page one in an eight-column feature strip.

No one mentioned it to me except Jo Ann, who came along and patted me on the head and said she was proud of me— although God knows why she should have been.

Then the Barnacle sent me out on another one of his wild-goose chases concerning someone who was supposed to be building a homemade atomic pile in his back yard. It turned out that this fellow is an old geezer who, at one time, had built a perpetual motion machine that didn't work. Once I found that out, I was so disgusted that I didn't even go back to the office, but went straight home instead.

I rigged up a block and tackle, had some trouble what with no one to help me, but I finally got the boat up on the blocks. Then I drove to a little village at the end of the lake and bought paint not only for the boat, but the cottage as well. I felt pretty good about making such a fine start on all the work I should do that fall.

The next morning when I got to the office, I found the place in an uproar. The switchboard had been clogged all night and it still looked like a Christmas tree. One of the operators had passed out, and they were trying to bring her to.

The Barnacle had a wild gleam in his eye, and his necktie was all askew. When he saw me, he took me firmly by the arm and led me to my desk and sat me down. "Now, damn you, get to work!" he yelled and he dumped a bale of notes down in front of me.

"What's going on?" I asked.

"It's that brownie deal of yours," he yelled. "Thousands of people are calling in. All of them have brownies; they've been helped by brownies; some of them have even seen brownies."

"What about the milk?" I asked.

"Milk? What milk?"

"Why, the milk they should set out for them."

"How do I know?" he said. "Why don't you call up some of the milk companies and find out?"

That is just what I did—and, so help me Hannah, the milk companies were slowly going crazy. Every driver had come racing back to get extra milk, because most of their customers were ordering an extra quart or so. They were lined up for blocks outside the stations waiting for new loads and the milk supply was running low.

There weren't any of us in the newsroom that morning who did anything but write brownie copy. We filled the paper with it—all sorts of stories about how the brownies had been helping people. Except, of course, they hadn't known it was brownies helping them until they read my story. They'd just thought that it was good luck.

When the first edition was in, we sat back and sort of caught our breath—although the calls still were coming in—and I swear my typewriter still was hot from the copy I'd turned out.

The papers came up, and each of us took our copy and started to go through it, when we heard a roar from J. H.'s office. A second later, J. H. came out himself, waving a paper in his fist, his face three shades redder than a brand-new fire truck.

He practically galloped to the city desk and he flung the paper down in front of the Barnacle and hit it with his fist. "What do you mean?" he shouted. "Explain yourself. Making us ridiculous!"

"But, J. H. I thought it was a good gag and—"

"Brownies!" J. H. snorted.

"We got all those calls," said Barnacle Bill. "They still are coming in. And—"

"That's enough," J. H. thundered. "You're fired!"

He swung around from the city desk and looked straight at me. "You're the one who started it," he said. "You're fired, too."

I got up from my chair and moved over to the city desk. "We'll be back a little later," I told J. H., "to collect our severance pay."

He flinched a little at that, but he didn't back up any.

The Barnacle picked up an ash tray off his desk and let it fall. It hit the floor and broke. He dusted off his hands. "Come on, Mark," he said; "I'll buy you a drink."

*

We went over to the corner. Joe brought us a bottle and a couple of glasses, and we settled down to business.

Pretty soon some of the other boys started dropping in. They'd have a drink or two with us and then go back to work. It was their way of showing us they were sorry the way things had turned out. They didn't say anything, but they kept dropping in. There never was a time during the entire afternoon when there wasn't someone drinking with us. The Barnacle and I took on quite a load.

We talked over this brownie business and at first we were a little skeptical about it, laying the situation more or less to public gullibility. But the more we thought about it, and the more we drank, the more we began to believe there might really be brownies. For one thing, good luck just doesn't come in hunks the way it appeared to have come to this town of ours in the last few weeks. Good luck is apt to scatter itself around a bit—and while it may run in streaks, it's usually prety thin. But here it seemed that hundreds—if not thousands—of persons had been visited by good luck.

By the middle of the afternoon, we were fairly well agreed there might be something to this brownie business. Then, of course, we tried to figure out who the brownies were, and why they were helping people.

"You know what I think," said Barnacle. "I think they're aliens. People from the stars. Maybe they're the ones who have been flying all these saucers."

"But why would aliens want to help us?" I objected. "Sure, they'd want to watch us and find out all they could; and after a while, they might try to make contact with us. They might even be willing to help us, but if they were they'd want to help us as a race, not as individuals."

"Maybe," the Barnacle suggested, "they're just busy-bodies. There are humans like that. Psychopathic do-gooders, always sticking in their noses, never letting well enough alone."

"I don't think so," I argued back at him. "If they are trying to help us, I'd guess it's a religion with them. Like the old friars who wandered all over Europe in the early days. Like the Good Samaritan. Like the Salvation Army."

But he wouldn't have it that way. "They're busy-bodies," he insisted. "Maybe they come from a surplus economy, a planet where all the work is done by machines and there is more than enough of everything for everyone. Maybe there isn't anything left for anyone to do—and you know yourself that a man has to have something to keep him occupied, something to do so he can think that he is important."

Then along about five o'clock Jo Ann came in. It had been her day off and she hadn't known what had happened until someone from the office phoned her. So she'd come right over.

She was plenty sore at me, and she wouldn't listen to me when I tried to explain that at a time like this a man had to have a drink or two. She got me out of there and out back to my car and drove me to her place. She fed me black coffee and finally gave me something to eat and along about eight o'clock or so she figured I'd sobered up enough to try driving home.

I took it easy and I made it but I had an awful head and I remembered that I didn't have a job. Worst of all, I was probably tagged for life as the man who had dreamed up the brownie hoax. There was no doubt that the wire services had picked up the story, and that it had made front page in most of the papers coast to coast. No doubt, the radio and television commentators were doing a lot of chuckling at it.

My cottage stands up on a sharp little rise above the lake, a sort of hog's back between the lake and road, and there's no road up to it. I had to leave my car alongside the road at the foot of the rise, and walk up to the place.

I walked along, my head bent a little so I could see the path in the moonlight, and I was almost to the cottage before I heard a sound that made me raise my head.

And there they were.

They had rigged up a scaffold and there were four of them on it, painting the cottage madly. Three of them were up on the roof replacing the bricks that had been knocked out of the chimney. They had storm windows scattered all over the place and were furiously applying putty to them. And you could scarcely see the boat, there were so many of them slapping paint on it.

I stood there staring at them, with my jaw hanging on my breastbone, when I heard a sudden *swish* and stepped quickly to one side. About a dozen of them rushed by, reeling out the hose, running down the hill with it. Almost in a shorter time than it takes to tell it, they were washing the car.

They didn't seem to notice me. Maybe it was because they were so busy they didn't have the time to—or it might have been just that it wasn't proper etiquette to take notice of someone when they were helping him.

They looked a lot like the brownies that you see pictured in the children's books, but there were differences. They wore pointed caps, all right, but when I got close to one of them who was busy puttying, I could see that it was no cap at all. His head ran up to a point, and that the tassle on the top of it was no tassle of a cap, but a tuft of hair or feathers—I couldn't make out which. They wore coats with big fancy buttons on them, but I got the impression—I don't know how—that they weren't buttons, but something else entirely. And instead of the big sloppy clown-type shoes they're usually shown as wearing, they had nothing on their feet.

They worked hard and fast; they didn't waste a minute. They didn't walk, but ran. And there were so many of them.

Suddenly they were finished. The boat was painted, and so was the cottage. The puttied, painted storm windows were leaned against the trees. The hose was dragged up the hill and neatly coiled again.

I saw that they were finishing and I tried to call them all together so that I could thank them, but they paid no attention to me. And when they were finished, they were gone. I was left standing, all alone—with the newly painted cottage shining in the moonlight and the smell of paint heavy in the air.

I suppose I wasn't exactly sober, despite the night air and all the coffee Jo Ann had poured into me. If I had been cold, stone sober I might have done it better; I might have thought of something. As it was, I'm afraid I bungled it.

I staggered into the house, and the outside door seemed a little hard to shut. When I looked for the reason, I saw it had been weather-stripped.

With the lights on, I looked around—and in all the time I'd been there the place had never been so neat. There wasn't a speck of dust on anything and all the metal shone. All the pots and pans were neatly stacked in place; all the clothing I had left strewn around had been put away; all the books were lined straight within the shelves, and the magazines were where they should be instead of just thrown anywhere.

I managed to get into bed, and I tried to think about it; but someone came along with a heavy mallet and hit me on the head and that was the last I knew until I was awakened by a terrible racket.

I got to it as fast as I could.

"What is it now?" I snarled, which is no way to answer a phone, but was the way I felt.

It was J. H. "What's the matter with you?" he yelled. "Why aren't you at the office? What do you mean by..."

"Just a minute, J. H.; don't you remember? you canned me yesterday."

"Now, Mark," he said, "you wouldn't hold that against me, would you? We were all excited..."

"*I* wasn't excited," I told him.

"Look," he said, "I need you. There's someone here to see you."

"All right," I said and hung up.

I didn't hurry any; I took my time. If J. H. needed me, if there was someone there to see me, both of them could wait. I turned on the coffee maker and took a shower; after the shower and coffee, I felt almost human.

I was crossing the yard, heading for the path down to the car, when I saw something that stopped me like a shot.

There were tracks in the dust, tracks all over the place—exactly the kind of tracks I'd seen in the flower bed underneath the window at the Clayborne estate. I squatted down and looked closely at them to make sure there was no mistake and there couldn't be. They were the self-same tracks.

They were brownie tracks!

I stayed there for a long time, squatting beside the tracks and thinking that now it was all believable because there was no longer any room for disbelief.

The nurse had been right; there had been something in the room that night Mrs. Clayborne died. It was a mercy, the old gardener said, his thoughts and speech all fuzzed with the weariness and the basic simplicity of the very old. An act of mercy, a good deed, for the old lady had been dying hard, no hope for her.

And if there were good deeds in death, there were as well in life. In an operation such as this, the surgeon had told me, there are so many factors that no one can take the credit. It was a miracle, he'd said, but don't you quote me on it.

And someone—no cleaning woman, but someone or something else—had messed up the notes of the physicist and in the messing of them had put together two pages out of several hundred—two pages that tied together and made sense.

Coincidence? I asked myself. Coincidence that a woman died and that a boy lived, and that a researcher got a clue he'd otherwise have missed? No, not coincidence when there was a track beneath a window and papers scattered from beneath a paperweight.

And—I'd almost forgotten—Jo Ann's old lady who sat rocking happily because all her old dead friends had come to visit her. There were even times when senility might become a very kindness.

I straightened up and went down to the car. As I drove into town I kept thinking about the magic touch of kindness from the stars or if, perhaps, there might be upon this earth, coexistent with the human race, another race that had a different outlook and a different way of life. A race, perhaps, that had tried time and time again to ally itself with the humans and each time had been rejected and driven into hiding—sometimes by ignorance and superstition and again by a too-brittle knowledge of what was impossible. A race, perhaps, that might be trying once again.

J. H. was waiting for me, looking exactly like a cat sitting serenely inside a bird cage, with feathers on his whiskers. With him was a high brass flyboy, who had a rainbow of decorations spread across his jacket and eagles on his shoulders. They shone so bright and earnestly that they almost sparkled.

"Mark, this is Colonel Duncan," said J. H. "He'd like to have a word with you."

The two of us shook hands and the colonel was more affable than one would have expected him to be. Then J. H. left us in his office and shut the door behind him. The two of us sat down and each of us sort of measured up the other. I don't know how the colonel felt, but I was ready to admit I was uncomfortable. I wondered what I might have done and what the penalty might be.

"I wonder, Lathrop," said the colonel, "if you'd mind telling me exactly how it happened.

"How you found out about the brownies?"

153

"I didn't find out about them, Colonel; it was just a gag."

I told him about the Barnacle shooting off his mouth about no one on the staff ever showing any initiative, and how I'd dreamed up the brownie story to get even with him. And how the Barnacle had got even with me by running it.

But that didn't satisfy the colonel. "There must be more to it than that," he said.

I could see that he'd keep at me until I'd told it, anyhow; and while he hadn't said a word about it, I kept seeing images of the Pentagon, and the chiefs of staff, and Project Saucer—or whatever they might call it now—and the FBI, and a lot of other unpleasant things just over his left shoulder.

So I came clean with him. I told him all of it and a lot of it, I granted, sounded downright silly.

But he didn't seem to think that it was silly. "And what do you think about all this?"

"I don't know," I told him. "They might come from outer space, or..."

He nodded quietly. "We've known for some time now that there have been landings. This is the first time they've ever deliberately called attention to themselves."

"What do they want, Colonel? What are they aiming at?"

"I wish I knew."

Then he said very quietly, "Of course, if you should write anything about this, I shall simply deny it. That will leave you in a most peculiar position at best."

I don't know how much more he might have told me—maybe quite a bit. But right then the phone rang. I picked it up and answered; it was for the colonel.

He said "Yes," and listened. He didn't say another word. He got a little white around the gills; then he hung up the phone.

He sat there, looking sick.

"What's the matter, Colonel?"

"That was the field," he told me. "It happened just a while ago. They came out of nowhere and swarmed all over the plane—polished it and cleaned it and made it spic and span, both inside and out. The men couldn't do a thing about it. They just had to stand and watch."

I grinned. "There's nothing bad about that, Colonel. They were just being good to you."

"You don't know the half of it," he said. "When they got it

154

all prettied up, they painted a brownie on the nose."

That's just about all there's to it as far as the brownies are concerned. The job they did on the colonel's plane was, actually, the sole public appearance that they made. But it was enough to serve their purpose if publicity was what they wanted—a sort of visual clincher, as it were. One of our photographers—a loopy character by the name of Charles, who never was where you wanted him when you wanted him, but nevertheless seemed to be exactly on the spot when the unusual or disaster struck—was out at the airport that morning. He wasn't supposed to be there; he was supposed to be covering a fire, which turned out luckily to be no more than a minor blaze. How he managed to wind up at the airport even he, himself, never was able to explain. But he was there and he got the pictures of the brownies polishing up the plane—not only one or two pictures, but a couple dozen of them, all the plates he had. Another thing—he got the pictures with a telescopic lens. He'd put it in his bag that morning by mistake; he'd never carried it before. After that one time he never was without it again and, to my knowledge, never had another occasion where he had to use it.

Those pictures were a bunch of lulus. We used the best of them on page one—a solid page of them—and ran two more pages of the rest inside. The AP got hold of them, transmitted them, and a number of other member papers used them before someone at the Pentagon heard about it and promptly blew his stack. But no matter what the Pentagon might say, the pictures had been run and whatever harm—or *good*—they might have done could not be recalled.

I suppose that if the colonel had known about them, he'd have warned us not to use them and might have confiscated them. But no one knew the pictures had been taken until the colonel was out of town, and probably back in Washington. Charlie got waylaid somehow—at a beer joint most likely—and didn't get back to the office until the middle of the afternoon.

When he heard about it, J. H. paced up and down and tore his hair and threatened to fire Charlie; but some of the rest of us got him calmed down and back into his office. We caught the pictures in our final street edition, picked the pages up for the early runs next day, and the circulation boys were pop-eyed for days at the way those papers sold.

The next day, after the worst of the excitement had subsided, the Barnacle and I went down to the corner to have ourselves a couple. I had never cared too much for the Barnacle before, but the fact that we'd been fired together established a sort of bond between us; and he didn't seem to be such a bad sort, after all.

Joe was as sad as ever. "It's them brownies," he told us, and he described them in a manner no one should ever use when talking of a brownie. "They've gone and made everyone so happy they don't need to drink no more."

"Both you and me, Joe," said the Barnacle; "they ain't done nothing for me, either."

"You got your job back," I told him.

"Mark," he said, solemnly, pouring out another. "I'm not so sure if that is good or not."

It might have developed into a grade-A crying session if Lightning, our most up-and-coming copy boy, had not come shuffling in at that very moment.

"Mr. Lathrop," he said, "there's a phone call for you."

"Well, that's just fine."

"But it's from New York," said the kid.

That did it. It's the first time in my life I ever left a place so fast that I forgot my drink.

The call was from one of the papers to which I had applied, and the man at the New York end told me there was a job opening in the London staff and that he'd like to talk with me about it. In itself, it probably wasn't any better than the job I had, he said, but it would give me a chance to break in on the kind of work I wanted.

When could I come in? he asked, and I said tomorrow morning.

I hung up and sat back and the world all at once looked rosy. I knew right then and there those brownies still were working for me.

I had a lot of time to think on the plane trip to New York; and while I spent some of it thinking about the new job and London, I spent a lot of it thinking about the brownies, too.

They'd come to Earth before, that much at least was clear.

156

And the world had not been ready for them. It had muffled them in a fog of folklore and superstition, and had lacked the capacity to use what they had offered it. Now they tried again. This time we must not fail them, for there might not be a third time.

Perhaps one of the reasons they had failed before—although not the only reason—had been the lack of a media of mass communications. The story of them, and of their deeds and doings, had gone by word of mouth and had been distorted in the telling. The fantasy of the age attached itself to the story of the brownies until they became no more than a magic little people who were very droll, and on occasion helpful, but in the same category as the ogre, or the dragon, and others of their ilk.

Today it had been different. Today there was a better chance the brownies would be objectively reported. And while the entire story could not be told immediately, the people could still guess.

And that was important—the publicity they got. People must know they were back again, and must believe in them and trust them.

And why, I wondered, had one medium-sized city in the midwest of America been chosen as the place where they would make known their presence and demonstrate their worth? I puzzled a lot about that one, but I never did get it figured out, not even to this day.

Jo Ann was waiting for me at the airport when I came back from New York with the job tucked in my pocket. I was looking for her when I came down the ramp and I saw that she'd got past the gate and was running toward the plane. I raced out to meet her and I scooped her up and kissed her and some damn fool popped a flash bulb at us. I wanted to mop up on him, but Jo Ann wouldn't let me.

It was early evening and you could see some stars shining in the sky, despite the blinding floodlights; from way up, you could hear another plane that had just taken off; and up at the far end of the field, another one was warming up. There were the buildings and the lights and the people and the great machines and it seemed, for a long moment, like a table built to represent the strength and swiftness, the competence and assurance of this world of ours.

Jo Ann must have felt it, too, for she said suddenly: "It's nice, Mark. I wonder if they'll change it."

I knew who she meant without even asking.

"I think I know what they are," I told her; "I think I got it figured out. You know that Community Chest drive that's going on right now. Well, that's what they are doing, too—a sort of Galactic Chest. Except that they aren't spending money on the poor and needy; their kind of charity is a different sort. Instead of spending money on us, they're spending love and kindness, neighborliness and brotherhood. And I guess that it's all right. I wouldn't wonder but that, of all the people in the universe, we are the ones who need it most. They didn't come to solve all our problems for us—just to help clear away some of the little problems that somehow keep us from turning our full power on the important jobs, or keep us from looking at them in the right way."

That was more years ago than I like to think about, but I still can remember just as if it were yesterday.

Something happened yesterday that brought it all to mind again.

I happened to be in Downing Street, not too far from No. 10, when I saw a little fellow I first took to be some sort of dwarf. When I turned to look at him, I saw that he was watching me; he raised one hand in an emphatic gesture, with the thumb and first finger made into a circle—the good, solid American signal that everything's okay.

Then he disappeared. He probably ducked into an alley, although I can't say for a fact I actually saw him go.

But he was right. Everything's okay.

The world is bright, and the cold war is all but over. We may be entering upon the first true peace the human race has ever known.

Jo Ann is packing, and crying as she packs, because she has to leave so many things behind. But the kids are goggle-eyed about the great adventure just ahead. Tomorrow morning we leave for Peking, where I'll be the first accredited American correspondent for almost thirty years.

And I can't help but wonder if, perhaps, somewhere in that

158

ancient city—perhaps in a crowded, dirty street; perhaps along the imperial highway; maybe some day out in the country beside the Great Wall, built so fearsomely so many years ago—I may not see another little man.

More top science fiction available from Magnum Books

T. J. Bass
413 3467 The Godwhale   65p

Alfred Bester
413 3457 Extro   60p

John Brunner
413 3458 The Wrong End of Time   55p

Philip K. Dick
413 3654 Dr Futurity   60p
413 3655 The Unteleported Man   50p
413 3653 The Crack in Space   70p
417 0197 The Simulacra   75p

Philip José Farmer
417 0100 Hadon of Ancient Opar   70p
417 0177 Flight to Opar   75p

Damon Knight
417 0220 Off Centre   70p
417 0222 In Deep   75p

Andrew J. Offutt
417 0190 Messenger of Zhuvastou   80p

Mack Reynolds
417 0178 Galactic Medal of Honour   75p

Clifford D. Simak
413 3690 Way Station   65p
413 3768 Time and Again   75p
413 3760 Cemetery World   70p
413 3695 Time is the Simplest Thing   70p
417 0171 A Choice of Gods   70p

These and other Magnum Books are available at your bookshop or newsagent. In case of difficulties orders may be sent to:

Magnum Books
Cash Sales Department
PO Box 11
Falmouth
Cornwall TR10 109EN

Please send cheque or postal order, no currency, for purchase price quoted and allow the following for postage and packing:

UK   19p for the first book plus 9p per copy for each additional book ordered, to a maximum of 73p.

BFPO   19p for the first book plus 9p per copy for the next 6 books, thereafter
& Eire   3p per book.

Overseas   20p for the first book and 10p per copy for each additional book.
customers

While every effort is made to keep prices low, it is sometimes necessary to increase prices at short notice. Magnum Books reserve the right to show new retail prices on covers which may differ from those previously advertised in the text or elsewhere.